I0741790

KINGPIN WIFEYS
VOLUME 1

BY

K. ELLIOTT

Copyright © 2013 by urban lifestyle press
P.O. Box 12714
Charlotte, nc 28220
http://www.kelliottonline.com/

Copyright 2013 by http://www.Kelliottonline.Com/.
All rights reserved.

No part of this book may be used or reproduced in any manner whatsoever without written permission. For information, address urban lifestyle press, p.O. Box 12714 charlotte, nc 28220 http://www.kelliottonline.com/

This ebook is licensed for your personal enjoyment only. This ebook may not be re-sold or given away to other people. If you would like to share this book with another person, please purchase an additional copy for each recipient. If you're reading this book and did not purchase it, or it was not purchased for your use only, then please return to amazon.Com and purchase your own copy. Thank you for respecting the hard work of this author.

November 2013

– PART ONE –

PART ONE

CHAPTER 1

Starr answered the blocked call, "Hello."

There was some deep breathing, followed by silence.

"Who the fuck is this, and why are you playing fucking games on my phone?"

More breathing.

She hung up.

The blocked number called again.

Starr said, "I'm going to call the fucking police if you call my phone again!" She terminated the call.

Seconds later she received a text from a number she didn't recognize—a 973 area code. The text said: *Calling the cops would be bad for business. I don't think your man would like that.*

Starr dialed the number. A recording said that the number was no longer in service. Weird.

She called Trey.

He didn't answer. She called him three more times. Finally he picked up.

"Hey babe."

"Hey babe my ass, you need to come home and come now."

"What's wrong? Are the police there?"

"No, the police are not here, Trey. Do you think I would ask you to come home if the police was here? Nobody is trying to set you up."

"I'm just saying whenever you're like come home and come home now, I think the worst."

Starr and Trey had been together for eight years. She met him when she was 21 and he was 31. She had been working at a cell phone store in the hood, and she noticed that he would always pull up in a different car, and he would change his cell phone every two weeks. Starr was a hood chick and she prided herself in having street smarts. She knew Trey was a baller; more importantly he wasn't cheap. When he would buy his phones, he'd always give her an extra hundred dollars. He said it was for being so cute.

She thought he was handsome, but she never thought she was his type until one day he asked.

"When are you going to go out with me?"

"When are you going to ask?"

Trey took her out that same night and when he dropped her off, he met her father, Ace, a 46-year-old ex con, who had done twelve years for moving weight. Ace approached the car and said, "Nigga, if you going to be dropping my daughter off, at least let me know who the fuck you are."

Then Trey introduced himself and called Ace sir.

"Kill that sir bullshit," Ace had demanded. From that day on, they had been good. Trey looked up to Ace like a father, and Ace would give him advice about the game. Ace didn't care if Trey was hustling but had warned him that the day he put his hands on his daughter would be the day that Trey died. Although Trey was no punk, he believed that Ace would in fact try to kill him, but he'd never hit a woman in his life.

Nine months later Starr moved in with Trey, and they had been together ever since.

"I'll be there in a couple of hours."

"Trey, come home now."

"In thirty minutes, I'm handling something."

She hung up the phone and called her girlfriend, Lani.

"Hey!"

"Yo, that blocked number called again."

Lani said, "Girl, you lying."

"I'm serious, girl, and the same thing happened like before, they were breathing hard and shit. I said I was going to call the police and I hung up. Seconds later I got a text and the text said that they knew I wasn't going to call the police, because it was bad for my man's business."

"Really?"

"Yes."

Lani said, "Girl, this shit is getting weird."

Starr said, "I know and I'm scared."

"Why?"

"I was just thinking it might be the Feds."

"No way."

"Why don't you think it's the Feds?"

"You think the Feds are going to call you and text you?"

"I guess you're right. Anyways, I don't want to talk about it anymore, at least not over the phone. Let's get together tomorrow for a mani and pedi, okay? How about going to Jada?"

Starr sighed, "Oh Lord, not the wanna-be model."

Lani said, "She's cool. Give her a chance."

"Your girl is as fake as that silicon ass she got. Talking 'bout how she's been doing squats, yeah right. Squats will not make your ass grow like that in one month. She got ass injections and she knows it."

Lani laughed, "Let that chile' think we believe that."

"Whatever."

When Starr hung up the phone, she heard Trey's Range Rover pull into the garage. Seconds later he entered the house with a Louis Vuitton duffel bag draped over his shoulder. He sat the bag on the floor and said "Count what's in the bag in the morning."

Trey wrapped his arms around her waist and said "Goddamn, baby. Why you looking so damn good. Why are you dressed up?"

Starr had forgotten she'd gotten dressed up. She had forgotten that she wanted to go to dinner with Trey. The anonymous caller was still on her mind.

Trey licked his lips and said, "It's going to be hard to talk about anything with that dress on." Starr knew the dress was a winner. She'd gotten it from a local designer, Acquan, who only made one piece per design. The dress was long and clung to her ass and it was backless. Starr's hair was up in a bun, her face revealed stunning cheekbones. She was average height and her curvy figure made men drool.

Starr said, "Let's talk."

"Okay."

She sat at the kitchen table and he grabbed a bottle of water from the fridge before sitting down across from her.

"What's up?"

"Been getting those weird phone calls again."

"Blocked numbers?"

"Yeah."

"I keep telling you to change your number."

"I ain't changing my number, Trey."

"Well what the fuck are we talking about this for then? What do you want me to do about it?"

"Trey, will you just shut up and listen."

He sat, quiet.

"Today I got a call, and I told them I was going to call the police. When I hung up the phone, I got a text."

Trey's eyes grew. "A text? What did it say?"

She passed him the phone. "It's the number that starts with 973." Trey read the text.

He said, "Did you call the number back?"

"The phone was disconnected."

Trey said, "Probably one of your jealous-ass friends. Somebody that you've put in our business."

"Trey, you know I don't talk and I don't brag."

"You don't have to talk. Posting pictures of our crib and our cars and shit on Facebook and Instagram. You know motherfuckers be hating. I don't know why you keep doing that dumb shit."

"Trey, I got my salon. I am a legitimate business owner."

"A salon that you don't ever run, you haven't been to the salon in eight months."

"What are you saying?"

"Look, babe, I'm just saying people get jealous and they play games."

"You think that's what this is?"

"I know how haters think. They want to make you feel as uncomfortable as possible."

She said, "I guess you're right." She stood and grabbed a bottle of water from the fridge then she picked up the bag and was about to head upstairs, but she turned to him and said, "But they said that the police wouldn't be good for your business. Hate is one thing but it's like this is a threat."

He walked over to her and she put her head in his chest. She liked when her head was against his chest. He was about a foot taller than her, and she liked that he made her feel small. He said, "Baby, nothing is going to happen to us."

He'd said that many times before, but he wasn't the corner hustler that she'd met many years ago. She had helped him count millions of dollars in cash and it was all his. She was nervous.

CHAPTER 2

LANI PULLED HER BMW X6 INTO THE GAS STATION PARKING LOT. A car behind her flicked its lights to get her attention. It was her ex-boyfriend, Black. She sat in the car with the heat blowing. It was freezing outside and the road was icy. She sure as hell knew that Black didn't want her to get out of the car to talk to him.

Black was just below six feet with a clean face except for a mustache. He was a well-built man with dreadlocks. He hopped in the passenger side of the car.

"Where you headed?" he asked.

"I'm headed home, and you?"

"Just left the South Side. You know, been working."

Lani knew what Black meant by working—he was a weed dealer. She'd known this man for 5 years and he sure as hell didn't have a real job, nor did he plan to get one. But that was okay with her. She liked men with money and didn't give a damn how they got it. Her new man dealt drugs, and she was okay with that as well.

He tried to rub her hand, but she pushed his hand away.

"What's your problem?" Black asked.

"Black, you know I got a man now."

Black frowned, "Now how the fuck are you going to treat me like this? We been knowing each other for years."

Lani turned her heat down and licked her lips. She was trying not to be angry. She didn't want to be in a bad mood when she got home. "Black, what part of 'I have a man' don't you understand?"

"I got it, but all I'm saying is we got history. I'm the one that moved your mom outta the projects. Paid for your brother's funeral cuz he didn't have insurance."

A tear trickled down her face because she felt indebted to Black, and she did care a lot for him, but she had a man now. She turned her head away, stared out the window for a second, then she faced him again. "You know, Black, I love you and I always will, but I have a man."

Black said, "Hey, I understand, but you don't have to treat me like I don't matter."

She yelled, "Stop it Black, stop trying to make me feel guilty, when it was you that fucked up! You went out and had not one, but two babies with two different bitches."

Black said, "Oh like you were perfect. You cheated on me too. You fucked O. Remember that."

"Yeah I fucked him and I admitted to it, but I only did it because you had bitches running up there to see you in jail. Nigga, I was faithful to you until you fucked up."

He reached for her hand again, this time she didn't push it away. Their eyes met and held. He said, "You were the best thing that ever happened to me, and I want you to be my wife. I want us to be together."

"You know I can't leave my man. He treats me so well."

"Does he love you though?"

"Yes."

"Cuz he buys you shit don't mean he loves you. The same shit you got from him, you can get from me and you'll get it with love."

She said, "Black, look, we're friends and we'll always be friends."

Black said, "I can't be your friend. I just can't. I love you."

She said, "I gotta go, Black."

He hopped out of her car.

She said, "Goodbye, Black."

He didn't respond, instead in hopped back into his car. She watched his white Porsche whizz out of the parking lot.

CHAPTER 3

DR. CRAIG MATTHEWS SIPPED A CARAMEL LATTE AS HE SAT IN THE back of Starbucks. He glanced at his watch. She was ten minutes late, he thought. He was checking his watch again for the third time in less than two minutes when she approached. A tall, gorgeous, black woman. He smiled bright then stood and hugged her and gave her a peck on the cheek.

He said, "What took you so long?"

"Had to do something for my mom. It took longer than I expected."

"Oh, glad you came."

"Of course."

"You look amazing," Dr. Matthews said.

His eyes glued to her, lusting after her very tiny waist and nice backside. A yellow and blue Gucci scarf draped her kissable neck. With teeth that were nice and beautiful, she was almost perfect. Her chin was a little off but he could fix that. He, after all, was the best cosmetic surgeon in Atlanta.

"I've been better, but I'm okay."

"How is the husband?"

"First of all I'm not married and how the fuck is your wife?" She tried to be polite and respectful with him, but sometimes she had to get ghetto with him and he seemed to respond well to it.

"Well, how is *his* business going?"

"Wait a fuckin' minute, Craig, can you kill the sarcasm? I mean everybody didn't have the money to go to med school like you, so don't fucking judge nobody. Don't say shit when I'm paying you with cash."

Craig was quiet for a moment, then said, "I just think you deserve better."

Jada was visibly irritated and she said, "And your wife deserves better than your cheating ass!"

"You leave my wife out of this!"

"And you leave my man out of this shit! What he does is his fucking business and don't you forget that."

His face and his eyes became sad. "I just don't want you to get caught up in his bullshit."

She was quiet for a moment, wondering how their relationship had grown to the point where she could talk to him about her man's business. Why did she trust him so much?

Craig said, "I'm sorry."

She said, "It's okay, I know you're right and I think about what ifs, all the time, but I just don't know what else I can do. I mean I'm thirty years old, and I don't have an education, so I don't know what I can do for money if something ever happened, or if I was to leave him."

Craig said, "I've always offered to take care of you."

She laughed and said, "I guess I could be your poor little black mistress. Is that what you want, Craig?"

"No. Well yes, but you don't have to put it that way."

"But then I'm back to square one, I still won't have anything of my own, I would be still counting on you to take care of me."

"But I earn legal money and business has just doubled. I am the best cosmetic surgeon in Atlanta."

She laughed, "Of course, that's why I came to you. I wanted you to make me perfecto."

Craig said, "You are perfect, you've always been perfect."

"Ahhh thank you. But I think I want my nose done next."

"Not by me. Really it's perfect."

She made a sad face.

"Thank you."

"So what does your man say when you say you want your nose done?"

"He says plastic surgery is for white bitches."

"His exact words?"

"Yeah but he loved my *butt* job."

Craig laughed. "I bet. I'm the best at what I do."

"But you're expensive as hell."

"Hey pay me, or pay some tranny from Craig's list to pump some super glue in your ass."

She said, "I guess you're right."

"Hey! My services ain't for the poor. But hell, your boyfriend ain't poor."

"Well he's doing okay."

"Must be. He always pays with cash. I hated counting all that cash."

"That's what you got employees for."

"Yeah but if they count it, they would have to report the transaction to the IRS."

"Really?"

"Yeah anything over 5 thousand has to get reported and believe me, you don't want those problems. I don't want those problems."

Her eyes met his eyes and she realized she liked him a lot. She didn't think he would ever do anything to hurt her. He was one of the few white men that she liked and somewhat trusted, and she thought he liked her, but it was getting a little scary. He wanted her to be his mistress. Was he serious? But she knew that if Shamari found out she was creeping with a white man, it could become ugly. Deadly serious. She had to be careful.

Her phone rang. She put her finger to her mouth. "Ssssh," she told Craig.

"Hello."

Shamari said, "What time you coming home, babe?"

"On my way back now."

"Stop at Chic-Fil-A and get me number one with lemonade."

"Okay." She stood and terminated the call and hugged Craig.

Craig said, "So when can we meet again."

She shrugged.

"I think we should go to Vegas again."

She said, "You know I can't get away again. You know he was out of the country the last time."

"Hell let's send him to Brazil."

She laughed.

He said, "I want to see you again."

She looked at Craig, knowing this man liked her. He didn't love her. She couldn't leave Shamari to be his mistress. Though she'd fucked Craig a few times, she didn't know if she could really be with him. She didn't know if she could be with any white man or any legitimate man for that matter. She liked what she liked and she liked bad boys.

• • •

Shamari was a tall, lanky light-complexioned man with a light beard. He planted a kiss on Jada's face when she came through the garage into the kitchen. His best friend Duke and a stranger, wearing a polo shirt exposing a tattoo sleeve, were sitting with him.

She hugged Duke, who was a tall muscular man with a pencil mustache and razor bumps. He'd been Shamari's best friend since they were kids.

"Jada," she said to the other man.

"I'm Tony."

"Tony, do you have a last name?"

"Tony Montana," the stranger said.

Shamari and Duke laughed.

Shamari said, "Babe, why so nosey?" Shamari always accused her of being nosey.

"Just want to know who's in my house, that's all."

"But who the fuck asks for people's government name except the government?" Shamari asked. He was always suspicious about people wanting to know too much even though she was his woman. He only wanted her to know so much.

"Okay, my bad," she placed the Chic-Fil-A food on the table and bolted upstairs before realizing she left her purse in the car. When she strolled through the kitchen, she heard Duke say, "I'm sure he's telling."

Tony said, "We don't have to keep talking about it, I'm going to handle the situation."

Shamari looked up at her before sipping his lemonade, shoving a handful of fries down his throat.

"Would you get outta here? Can't you see men talking?"

"Left my purse in the car. I could care less what y'all are talking about." She eased into the garage.

She retrieved her purse then stood in front of the door entrance and eavesdropped.

Shamari said, "Nobody gets hurt but him."

Tony said, "Whatever you say. I'll do the job however you want. If you want me to kill the roaches I will kill the roaches. I work for you. I will do the job anyway you want me to do it"

Shamari said, "No kids and no women."

Tony said, "Whatever you say boss, since I'm going to have my mask on I will just put the kids and the girl in one room and pop him."

Shamari said, "Good deal."

Tony said, "If she doesn't cooperate, I'm going to have to pop her too."

"But only if she don't do what you say," Shamari said.

Duke said, "This dude should have been dead a long time ago. You remember when he shorted eleven stacks?"

Shamari said, "I don't want to hear that could-have would-have shit. We gotta job to do now, because he said I knew something about those thirty kilos they found in the trunk of his Jag, I'm gonna get life with my record."

Tony said, "I'm the equalizer. Even if he did, he won't live to testify."

Shamari gave Tony a pound.

Tony said, "So where is my money?"

Shamari said to Duke, "Give him the thirty thousand."

Tony said, "I only wanted twenty-five."

Shamari said, "But I trust that you're going to handle this the right way. So take an extra five."

Tony said, "I'm a professional."

CHAPTER 4

LANI'S BOYFRIEND, CHRIS, LOVED BASKETBALL AND HE'D BEEN A ballplayer before he started hustling full-time, after his mother's home was foreclosed. He was 6'5 two hundred and twenty-five pounds. He and Lani had floor seats for the Hawks game. They were playing the Lakers tonight, and he and Lani were there with the rest of the who's who of Atlanta trying to be seen. At the game Lani wore an electric blue dress that exposed just a hint of her back. Her hair flowed and her six-inch heels elevated that ass and made it look spectacular.

Chris was rubbing Lani's thigh when he noticed a man with floor seats on the other side of the arena looking his way.

"What the fuck is that character looking at?"

Lani turned to Chris, "What are you talking about?"

"The man across the court in the red shirt. Sitting there next to the clown with the Mohawk," Chris said, "I mean I can see if he was checking you out, but that dude is looking at me, Lani."

Lani recognized Black and his friend Kyrie.

"Baby, I think you're overreacting. Nobody is looking at you."

Black had turned his attention back to the game.

"I'm telling you, he was watching me."

"Baby, just watch the game. He probably thinks you're a basketball player or something."

Chris said, "Maybe." Since he was tall he had often been mistaken for a basketball player. Sometimes a football player.

Lani held his hand trying not to look at Black. Damn, she'd never known Black to like basketball. Boxing maybe. What the fuck was he doing here and why was he looking in her direction. She watched the game avoiding Black's gaze.

Later Chris and Lani were standing at the concession stand getting drinks, and on the way back to their seats Black bumped Chris, knocking one of the drinks to the floor.

"What the fuck?" Chris said.

Black smiled and said, "My bad partna."

Lani didn't know what to say. She didn't want to speak to Black but this was a man she'd known for ten years.

Black said, "Hey Lani."

Chris said, "You know this clown?"

Black said, "Let me buy you some more drinks partna." He grinned again. "Seriously, it was an accident."

Chris said, "This is the nigga that was staring at us. Now I know why he was staring. He knows you."

Black still grinning said, "Lani, you ain't gonna speak?"

"Black don't start no bullshit. I ain't got time for this."

Chris doused Black with the other drink.

Seconds later the two men locked like a couple of pit bulls, neither having a clear advantage.

Black said, "You bitch ass nigga, let go of my shirt and fight like a man."

Security came and separated them.

Seconds later, police officers were at the scene. They cuffed both men and led them away.

Lani said, "Baby, I'm going to call the bondsman."

Black grinned and said, "Thanks, babe."

"Nigga, I ain't talking about you," Lani said.

Kyrie said to Lani, "I'm sorry. I told that fool he was out of bounds. But, Lani, you gotta understand that Black loves you. He ain't over you yet."

Lani said, "He might as well be over me, I can never get back with him. I have a man that loves me."

Kyrie said, "Black will always love you."

Lani said, "I don't want to hear that bullshit, I got to get my man out of jail and I gotta get him out fast. Fuck Black."

She left the arena and called a bail bondsman.

CHAPTER 5

SHAMARI'S CELL PHONE RANG IN THE MIDDLE OF THE NIGHT. HE picked it up on the second ring. Jada rolled over and glanced at the clock on the dresser. It was 2:45 am

"Who the fuck is that? Calling this time of the morning!"

"Don't worry about it. Go back to bed."

Jada said, "Let me see that phone." It had better not be Rachel Hernandez, the bitch that she'd caught Shamari leaving the W hotel with a few months ago. She listened for a moment; she could tell it was a man's voice—sounded like Tony. She folded her pillow in half and tried to resume her rest, but she couldn't. She thought about what she heard when she was in the garage. The hit they'd planned. Why in the hell was he calling? Why couldn't it have waited until the morning?

Shamari said, "Did something go wrong?"

"Yeah, real wrong."

"Where are you?"

"Bruh, I'm in the woods. I'm hiding; the police are all over the place. They are searching for me. They got the helicopters out and everything.

"Get rid of that cell phone."

"I know! I gotta get out of these woods first, I think I can make it. I need to make it out before the dogs get a trail on me. I'm approaching somebody's house. I can see a man on the porch. An old black man. I'm hoping he'll let me stay there till the morning."

"If he don't?"

"If he don't, I'm fucked and just get me an attorney and take care of my babies."

"I got you man."

Tony said, "Appreciate you bruh."

Shamari sprang from the bed and eased out into the hallway, trying to walk as lightly as possible. He paced the hallway then turned to see Jada. "You scared me babe, why are you not in bed?"

"What's wrong with you?"

"Nothing."

"Yeah right, you know I know you."

He embraced her, and said, "If something happens to me, just know I love you."

"What's going to happen to you?"

"I don't really wanna get into it right now."

Jada said, "Tony, he's in trouble right?"

"What?" He looked shocked. Trying to figure out how she'd guessed that it had something to do with Tony.

"I recognized his voice; I'll never forget that voice." She still held his hand. "What happened?"

He looked her in the eyes. "You remember Don?"

"Yeah?"

"He got busted a few months ago and now he's talking?"

"Huh?"

"Talking to the cops. Snitching. How else do you want me to say it?"

"How you know?"

"When he got out on bond I met him and he kept talking about old stuff that had happened years ago."

"Had a wire on him." Jada said, "That motherfucker. All the times you've helped his bitch ass out. Bought his kids clothes and everything. Gave him money."

"I'm sure."

She thought about Craig. For that moment she thought being his mistress wouldn't be a bad idea after all, at least she couldn't go to jail for being a mistress.

"And you sent Tony to take care of him?"

He didn't want to admit that to her or nobody for that matter.

"I listened from the garage. I heard you tell him not to hurt anybody but Don."

"Don't repeat that to nobody, the less you know the better."

"You know I would do nothing to hurt you."

She followed him back to the kitchen. "You gonna tell me what happened?"

"He didn't say over the phone. He just said something went bad."

"Where is he?"

"In the woods somewhere in Gwinnett County."

"Damn, you think he's going to be okay?"

"I hope so."

She took a deep breathing then said, "I was just thinking about Tiffany and the kids."

Tiffany was Don's wife. She and Jada weren't exactly friends but they were cool with each other.

"I think they're fine."

"You hope so, you mean?"

He banged his fist against the table. "Why you gotta be so goddamned negative? I hated I had to do that, but I had to, he was trying to take my life away."

She made herself a cup coffee with a cream and two sugars, sipped it and said, "Damn."

He stared her in the eye and said, "It's real fucked up right now."

At 6:17 the doorbell rang. Tony stood on the front porch wearing soiled jeans and a ripped t-shirt in 27 degree weather.

He followed Shamari to the kitchen. They sat at the kitchen table. "What the fuck happened?"

Tony said, "It went all bad, man. All bad." His eyes were moist. He wanted to cry.

Shamari said, "Dude what the fuck happened?"

"I kicked the door in and Don fired first, which shocked the hell out of me. I wasn't expecting him."

Shamari said, "Well you did kick his door in."

Tony said, "Then I fired, then his wife came running out of another room, so I aimed and shot her."

"Damn, I told you nobody but Don."

"I know, man, but I thought she was a dude, man."

"Did you get Don?"

"I fired, but I don't know if I hit him."

Not only did this idiot hit the wrong person, but he didn't even know if he'd killed the right person. There was a possibility that Don was still living. Shamari stood up from the table. He wanted to pace, but this info was crippling. He just stood there thinking about prison; two of his brothers were there and one of his uncles as well. That was not somewhere he wanted to be. At that moment he regretted sending dumb ass Tony on a mission, clearly he wasn't as qualified as he had led him to believe.

Tony said, "That's not all."

"What else happened?"

"A little girl looking to be around 9 or 10 came out of her bedroom and I shot. Man I don't know why, but I was nervous." Tony began to cry, "I didn't mean to do it man," Tony said, with a stupid- ass look on his face. "It just kind of happened, you know."

"No, I don't know!" Shamari banged his fist against the table and said, "Goddamn it, you did exactly what I told you not to do!"

"I'm sorry." Tony's face got serious. "I've always gone to jail alone and this time it will be no different, I'm gonna wear it if I have to."

Shamari believed Tony. Tony had done 15 years in the Fed. He'd gotten caught with ten kilos of cocaine that wasn't his and he didn't talk, but this was bigger. This was attempted murder on a government informant. There was a difference. Stakes were higher. Both of their lives were on the line.

Jada burst in the kitchen, "Man the news have been showing that shit all morning."

Tony stared at her. He looked uneasy.

Shamari said, "She knows everything, I told her."

Jada said, "The eleven-year-old, Essence, died and a woman who was in the house is in critical condition.

"Damn, we're fucked."

Tony said, "I swear to you Shamari, I ain't going out like that. You don't have anything to worry about. This is all on me."

Shamari said, "We gotta get you outta here. Do you have anywhere to go?"

Tony said, "I need some clothes and some money, and if you give me a bus ticket to Baltimore I will be fine once I get there."

Shamari said, "I paid you already."

Tony said, "My wife and kids is going to need that money."

Shamari sighed.

Tony became irritated with Shamari's unwillingness to give him some money. He said, "Now if you want me to keep my mouth shut, give me the money."

Jada said, "Ok, do Shamari have something to worry about?"

Tony looked at Shamari, not even acknowledging that Jada was in the room. "Look I know that sounded fucked up but I didn't mean it that way. I just need to get to Baltimore. If you can't, I understand. You did pay me."

Shamari said, "I'll get you the ticket, and I'll give you ten stacks."

"That's all I need. Once I get where I'm going, I'll be okay; I'll be able to hustle up some money to take care of myself once I'm there."

"Cool." Shamari said.

CHAPTER 6

TREY TOLD STARR, "YOU'RE THE BEST THING THAT EVER HAPPENED to me." They lay in the bed, silk sheets barely covering both of their naked bodies.

Starr smiled, not because Trey had just put it down in bed, but because of the nice things he always said to her. He always made her feel so lucky. Not only was her man super generous to her, but he loved her. Something many women didn't have. They usually had one or the other. Starr gave Trey a peck on the cheek and then scooted her butt against him. She could feel his throbbing dick against her ass and she loved it. Moments later she grabbed it and eased it into her lovehole. She came three times before he pulled out and came all over her ass. She turned to him and frowned.

"What's wrong babe?"

"You always do that."

"Do what?"

"You know, I want you to come inside me."

"I know, babe, but not yet. I will when I get out the game, babe. I don't want to be raising kids while I'm in the game."

She sat up on the edge of the bed pulled the sheet up to her chin. She looked sad and he didn't like it.

He scooted beside her and started massaging her back. Then he said, "Baby, we're going to have a baby one day. Just not right now."

She turned to him and said, "You always say that. You've been saying that for years."

He continued to massage her. He kissed her neck then he placed his scruffy face on her shoulder. She winced a little but she didn't move.

Starr forced a smile then said, "So when do you think you'll be done?"

He said, "Soon babe, real soon, As soon as Derringer blows up. I'm out of this game."

Derringer was a hip rapper he'd been trying to make into a household name. He'd invested a half a million dollars in Derringer's rap career.

"You've been saying that for the past two summers. Have you ever thought that maybe Derringer ain't got what it takes?"

Trey said, "This is ATL. All we gotta do is get the strip clubs to start playing his shit and it can catch on."

She said, "The strip clubs have been playing his shit and it ain't catching on."

Trey said, "Derringer is the best lyricist in ATL beside Andre 3000."

Starr said, "Trey don't nobody give a damn about lyrics. I know I don't and my girls damn sure don't. We want to dance. When I buy music, I buy it cause it's catchy and has a nice beat."

Trey looked sad, he said, "You right."

Starr kissed Trey and said, "Baby, I just don't want us starting our family dependent on Derringer getting a hit, cuz I don't see that shit happening."

Trey said, "I just don't want to get you pregnant knowing that I don't have something legitimate. I don't want to be looking over my shoulders."

Starr said, "Babe, I've helped you count millions of dollars. We have enough money. We can live off ten grand a month and be comfortable."

"And ordinary."

"And what's wrong with being ordinary?"

"I just don't want my kid to have to want for nothing."

Starr said, "Bullshit, Trey, I think you're addicted to the power."

He pulled a little bit of sheet from her and got underneath and said, "You might be right."

She said, "I know I'm right."

They kissed again. Before long he was inside her again. Missionary. Twenty minutes later he came again. This time he sprayed her chest.

CHAPTER 7

IT WAS 9:33 AM WHEN CHRIS GOT BAILED OUT. LANI WAS WAITING for him in front of the police station. He hopped on the passenger side of the Range Rover.

"So what the fuck is up with you and Black?"

"Oh, Chris, it's too early in the morning for this bullshit. Okay? Can we just get home before we start arguing?"

"Why didn't you tell me that your fuckin' ex was staring at me?"

"Because I knew you were going to act just like you're acting now. Like a fucking child."

"What the fuck ever. That dude knew who I was and I ain't even know who he was, that's some bullshit, Lani, and you know it."

She pulled her BMW onto the side of the road and said, "Look, Chris, I'm sorry. I should have handled it better. I didn't handle it like a real woman was supposed to and I'm sorry."

Chris said, "Are you still fuckin this dude?"

Lani said, "Oh my God, here come the high school ass questions. You think I'm that fuckin' trifling? I've never been the type of chick to fuck with two dudes."

Chris said, "I don't get it. What was that all about?"

Lani said, "I will admit, Black still has feelings for me, and I love him too and always will, but I'm not in love with him. I'm in love with you. But I can't erase Black and our past. If I could, I would because you're my man."

"Look Lani, I believe you but what is this nigga's problem?"

Lani said, "When Black and I broke up, he said I would be nothing without him, and that I would never find anybody that treated me like he treated me. And now it seems as though I upgraded and it's killing him to see me doing great without him."

Chris said, "I swear to you Lani, I will kill Black's ass if he ever puts his goddamned hands on me again. So if you want the man that you still love to live, you better tell him to stay the fuck away from me. I ain't nobody to play with."

Lani said, "Look I'm going to talk to his Nana, she'll calm his ass down. She raised him and she is the only one who he will listen to and Nana loves me."

"You better say something to that nigga or else Nana will be lowering his ass down - *In the fucking ground.*"

CHAPTER 8

STARR, LANI, AND JADA MET AT THE RA SUSHI BAR. THEY SAT AT THE back of the restaurant, in a booth, while they chatted over lobster rolls and salmon. Starr said, "This whole anonymous caller bullshit has got me thinking."

Lani said, "Thinking about what?"

Starr grabbed a lobster roll and said, "Thinking about if this bullshit is worth it, I mean that text kind of scared me, I don't want to go to jail. I want my man to get out the game, start something legitimate so we can start a family."

Lani said, "Why don't y'all just start a family anyway?"

Starr said, "That's exactly what I said, but Trey said it would be selfish until he can go legitimate."

Jada said, "I thought Trey had a record label?"

Starr said, "So does every other big time dope boy in Atlanta. You know that shit ain't nothing but a front." She looked at Jada. She really didn't like Jada but didn't think Jada was so stupid that she didn't know most record labels were fronts for drug dealers. Starr then said, "I'm sure your man has some kind of front."

Jada said, "Not really, he's thinking about opening up a clothing store, but he's been saying that for a while."

Lani said, "My man doesn't want to do anything but keep stacking money."

Starr said, "What does Chris tell the neighbors? They have to be wondering. You know how white folks are; they want to know everything about you so they can start googling you and shit."

Lani said, "The funny thing is, Chris is very personable. They don't ask him shit. I think they assume he's an ex-athlete cuz he's so tall."

Starr said, "Well the white man next door came over as soon as we moved in the neighborhood with some bullshit fruit basket asking a whole lot of questions."

Jada said, "What did you tell him?"

"Trey said he was a music producer. Said he made beats for Diddy."

Jada laughed.

Starr said, "After that, we didn't have any more problems but we don't have a lot of company, so shit is real cool with us and our neighbors. They invite us over all the time. Sometimes we go. Sometimes we don't."

Lani said, "I need you to relax, sissy. Nothing is going to happen. Don't put negative energy in the universe and nothing will happen."

Starr said, "I know, but I've been doing this for so long. I'm just so tired of this game. I know I got the luxuries but sometimes I'd rather just have my man. Sometimes the game can drain you. You know, moving cuz somebody got busted, being scared that you're going to get ratted, the prison visits. Trey and I went to visit his friend Terry, and let me tell you that's some sad shit."

Jada said, "I visit my brother in prison, so I know first-hand."

Starr said, "The saddest part about it is the kids running around happy to see their daddies. It's happy and sad."

Lani said, "Let's talk about something positive. I don't want that energy out there. I love my life and I ain't giving it up for nobody."

Jada said, "I can relate to Starr, I'm tired of the bullshit that comes with it."

Lani said, "So what are you going to do? Leave and then what? Go back to school? Bitches y'all asses is almost thirty. If you were smart, you would be stashing some of that money and start your own shit.

Jada said, "I don't have to be with Shamari, I got other options."

Lani said, "You better stay away from that married man cuz if his wife finds out, your ass is grass and if Shamari finds out, you finished bitch, believe that."

Jada knew what they were saying was true. She'd just witnessed Shamari put a hit out on somebody.

Starr rolled her eyes at Jada and said, "A married man?"

Jada said, "It's not what you think."

Starr said, "That's one thing I don't like. I don't like bitches that will fuck a married man."

Jada said, "Who said I fucked him?" Knowing damn well she'd fucked him on more than one occasion.

Lani said, "She's just getting his bread."

Starr said, "Same thing. And why does she need to get his money. Her man has money."

Jada said, "Don't judge me."

Starr said, "I'm not judging you, but I know I can't trust you around my man."

Jada said, "I've been around your man, and I don't want him. I have a man that treats me very well."

Lani could sense that this was getting out of hand. She said, "Both of y'all chill".

Starr said, "I'm good."

Jada smiled and said, "Me too."

They finished eating but Jada didn't say anything else to Starr.

CHAPTER 9

THE DOORBELL RANG AND WHEN SHAMARI OPENED THE DOOR HE was surprised to see Tony. He invited him in then frisked him. Tony was supposed to be on his way to Baltimore. Not here.

Tony said, "No wires... yet."

Shamari said, "What the hell does that mean?"

"Means I need you to give me thirty more thousand dollars, Big-Boy."

"What the fuck? You agreed to a price!" Shamari walked into the kitchen and Tony followed.

He offered him a glass of water.

Tony said, "You wouldn't happen to have a beer?"

"No, I've got soda."

"Give me one." Shamari passed him a coke and said, "You agreed to this price Tony. This is bullshit homie!"

Tony said, "I can't go to Baltimore."

"Why?"

"The police are already on my ass. They know it was me."

"What?"

Tony said, "Cameras in front of a convenience store around the corner from the scene of the crime got my license plate. I had stopped there for gas earlier."

"Cut it out."

Jada entered the kitchen and said, "I saw it on the news."

Shamari said, "What the fuck? Why didn't you tell me?"

Jada said, "I was gonna tell you but you were asleep last night after the news went off."

Tony said, "Come on man, thirty thousand is nothing to you."

Shamari became visibly angry. He said, "You blackmailing me?"

Tony lifted his shirt revealing a chrome handgun and said, "Look, nigga, give me the fuckin money. I'm sure you don't want it to get ugly in this motherfucker."

Jada said, "Give him the money, babe, this ain't worth it."

Tony smiled at Jada. "This Barbie looking bitch does have sense, I underestimated you." He grinned

Shamari said, "Dude, don't disrespect my lady."

Tony took a swig of his coke and said, "Dude, gimme the bread and I'm out."

Shamari said to Jada, "Count thirty grand."

Tony said, "Make it forty."

Shamari stared at Tony and Tony said, "I got 4 kids who ain't gonna see their daddy any more. Wouldn't you agree that's worth another ten thousand?"

Shamari said, "Dude, you act like this shit is my fault."

"It's not your fault but it was your idea. Your boy didn't snitch on me, now did he?" Tony said then he finished off his can of coke.

Jada came back with a designer backpack. She passed the money to Tony. He grabbed another can of coke and bumped his chest and said, "Death before dishonor nigga." He sprinted out the door.

CHAPTER 10

THE TEXT MESSAGE WAS FROM A 305 AREA CODE AND IT SAID, "YOU think your life is so fucking good. I hate you bitch."

Starr dialed the number and the recording said: *You have reached a number that is no longer in service.* She tried again and got the same recording. She called Trey.

"Hello."

"Got another text message from someone saying they hate me."

"What was the number?"

"It was a Miami area code and when I dialed the number. The recording said that I had reached a number that was no longer in service."

Trey said, "It must be some kind of app."

"Yeah, I think you're right."

Trey said, "This shit is getting fucking weird."

"I know babe, I know."

"Change your number for me."

Starr said, "I really didn't want to."

"Why not?"

"I love this number, it's easy for people to remember."

Trey said, "People don't remember numbers anymore."

Starr said, "I just don't want to change my number."

Trey said, "Well please don't tell me nothing else about these calls then, I don't want to hear about it."

"There is somebody out there that knows all of our fucking business, and you don't give a damn huh?"

"You're right, I don't give a damn. And I don't want to talk about this shit over the phone."

"Well you need to come home so we can talk."

"Look, you know I'm working. Can you talk to somebody else right now? Call Lani, you put that bitch in all of our business anyway."

"Whatever Trey. I'll see you tonight."

"And please have some food prepared. I am tired of takeout."

"Whatever nigga." She hung the phone up.

• • •

Lani and Chris were about to back out of her mother's driveway when a black Benz blocked her in. She dropped her head and said, "Oh God, its Black."

Chris unbuttoned his seat belt and said, "I've had enough of this clown." He bounced from the car.

Black got out of the Benz and smiled and said, "Hey, bruh, how are you doing?"

Chris said, "Motherfucker, you don't know me."

"You right, I don't know you." He extended his hand. "I'm Black."

Chris refused the handshake. "Dude, we ain't friends. We will never be friends."

Chris said, "Babe, pop the trunk."

Black brandished a nine millimeter and said, "Dude, I'm here to make peace. You know what I mean? Peace as in no violence or blowing your fucking brain to pieces right here in the goddamned drive way. You pick the kind of peace you want."

Lani got out of the car and said, "Ain't gonna be no shit in front of my mama's house."

Black said, "I just wanted to talk to him."

Lani said, "Black you need to leave."

"Have you forgotten who made the down payment on this house?"

Chris said, "I'll give you your money back, clown. What we owe you? Twenty racks?"

Lani's mom opened the door and peeked out.

Black said, "Hey, Miss Carolyn." He tucked his gun back down into his pants. Carolyn smiled and said, "Hey, Tyrann, how you been baby?" Lani's mother always called him Tyrann, she refused to call him by his nickname. Only two people called him Tyrann, Miss Carolyn and Nana.

Black said excuse me and hopped onto the porch and planted a kiss on Carolyn's jaw then said, "Im'ma send somebody over here to pressure wash this driveway."

"Oh, baby, you so sweet," Carolyn said then she said to Lani, "I'm going back in here to finish watching my Lifetime movies. I'll call you tomorrow."

"Bye, Mama."

Black said to Chris. "I just wanna talk, I didn't come to fight."

Chris said, "Okay, talk."

"I just want you to know that you got a good woman."

Chris didn't respond.

"And I'm still in love with her and I want her back."

Chris removed his jacket and he paused and said, "You know what? If you didn't have that fucking gun, I would beat the brakes off you."

Black said, "But I do, so you can't." Black hopped in his car and said, "I'm going to get my woman back," and he screeched off.

Then, Chris and Lani hopped into the car and took off.

CHAPTER 11

JADA SAID, "I JUST SAW ON THE NEWS THAT THEY CAUGHT TONY."
Shamari said, "You're bullshitting right?"
"No, they caught him in Miami. At one of his kid's mother's home."
"I didn't know that he had a child in Miami."
Jada said, "Apparently."
"Damn."
"I know right." She paced around the room.
He said, "Would you sit down! You're making me fucking nervous."
She was irritated with his tone, but she could see why it would make him nervous.
Jada said, "He's going to tell ain't he?"
Shamari said, "I don't know." He stood and paced. He knew Tony had been a standup guy but his last case was a drug possession. This was first-degree murder and attempted murder on a witness. He really didn't know how Tony would hold up."
Jada said, "Call your lawyer."
"I haven't been charged with anything yet."
"But you should be ready, just in case."
Shamari said, "I'm going to get the fuck away for a while.
"Where you going and what the hell am I going to do. I'm going with you."
He stared at her and said, "You don't need to be with me. I don't want anything to happen to you. I can handle myself. Believe that."

She said, "Okay, but what the hell am I supposed to do to support myself and how long are you gonna be away."

He said, "As long as I need to be away." He opened his bottom drawer and started slinging underwear and socks. Then he said, "Take a hundred grand from the stash. That should hold you for a while."

She said, "Thanks, but you know you should really wait till tomorrow. You don't know what's going on."

He closed the drawer and said, "I gotta calm myself down."

She said, "Now you're talking sense." She'd never seen that side of him. Normally he was so hard, but she figured the thought of life in the can would make anybody turn into a bitch. Everybody wants to shine, but nobody wants to do the time.

He said, "I will wait till the morning."

She said, "I think you should."

• • •

Twenty minutes after Trey left, the doorbell rang. Starr pulled the curtains back. A thick blond with fake boobs and a spray on tan stood on the porch. Starr said, "Hey I'm not interested in buying anything."

The woman said, "Starr, can you open the door for a moment. I need to talk."

Starr wondered how the woman knew her name. She opened the door and invited the woman in.

The blond smiled and said, "I'm Jessica Turner."

Starr looked puzzled but she said, "Nice to meet you."

Jessica smirked and said, "I don't think you're going to mean that once I tell you why I'm here."

Starr said, "What the hell are you talking about?"

Jessica smiled and said, "The anonymous calls you'd been receiving and the text messages. That was me."

"What the fuck was that all about?" Starr said forgetting all about the proper voice she used around white folks.

"There is something you need to know."

Starr said, "I know you need to get the fuck out of my house." She opened the door.

Jessica said, "I will leave, but I want you to know that I have a child from Trey."

Starr stood there stunned. What the fuck did the bitch just say?

"Yeah, Lil' Trey is about to be five."

"Bitch, you're delusional. Trey ain't got no kids, and he damn sure don't like white bitches."

Jessica said, "No, you're delusional. The DNA came back 99.999 % five years ago. I still have a copy of it."

Starr walked into the living room and invited Jessica. When they were seated, Starr said, "Now please tell me you're playing games."

Jessica said, "Why would I want to play games with you?"

"Why are you just now telling me this shit? You obviously knew who I was."

Jessica turned from Starr's gaze and said, "Does it matter when I told you? What difference does it make?"

"You know what, I don't believe you. I'm calling Trey." She dialed his number, Trey answered on the first ring.

"Trey, bring yo ass home right now."

"Babe, I'm working, I don't have time to be talking about no weird phone calls."

"I know who's been making the calls now."

Trey said, "Who?"

"Jessica."

"Who the hell is that?"

"Yo baby's mama, that's who!"

"I'm on my way home."

The doorbell rang again.

Jessica said, "That's probably my mother."

"You brought your Mom with you?"

"Yup and Trey Jr."

Jessica trailed Starr to the door and Starr let Jessica's mom and Trey Jr. in.

Jessica said, "This is Starr, Trey's girlfriend."

Starr shook the older woman's hand. Though she didn't care for her daughter's foolishness, she saw no reason to be disrespectful to her mother. Then she smiled at Trey Jr.

Jessica said, "Trey, say hi to Miss..." she looked at Starr.

"Coleman is my last name. Starr Coleman."

Starr shook Trey Jr.'s hand .The damn boy was a spitting image of his father, except he was lighter.

They all headed back into the living room. Starr offered them drinks and they all wanted water, so she disappeared to the kitchen and brought back some bottled water. As soon as she handed them the water, Trey stormed in.

Trey Jr. grabbed his father by the leg and said, "Daddy."

Trey ran his finger through his son's hair looking dumb as hell. Starr couldn't believe this shit. She really wanted to curse his ass out, and if it wasn't for the old woman and the kid, she would have surely went off.

Trey planted a kiss on T. J.'s forehead.

Trey Jr. said, "Daddy, are we going to play catch again like we did last time?"

Jessica said, "T. J., I'm surprised you remember that. It's been what, like six months, Trey."

"Yeah, I remember and we had ice cream."

Trey said, "Yes, we're going to play catch again. Mrs. Robinson, can you take Trey into the den?" He pointed and said, "It's down the hall and to the right."

The old woman said, "Yes." She stood and said, "Come on T. J."

When Mrs. Robinson and the kid were gone, Trey said to Jessica, "What the fuck are you doing here?"

Starr said, "No, why the fuck didn't I know about this, Trey? What the fuck is going on?"

Trey ignored Starr and said, "Why are you here?"

Jessica said, "Because this is the only way I can get you to see your son. You fuckin' loser."

Starr said, "So, Trey, you gonna act like I ain't even here?"

Trey said, "Chill, babe, let me handle this."

Jessica said to Starr, "This dude is a fuckin loser, he's a loser, I'm telling you."

Trey said, "I'm a loser, cuz I don't fuck you."

Jessica said, "Dude, I don't want you, I just want you to do right."

Trey said, "You just text me last week trying to get me to come over and fuck you, and you're just mad that I'm loyal to my girl."

Jessica laughed a loud laugh. "You're loyal to your girl alright. Is that how come I got pregnant?"

A tear rolled down Starr's face. Trey tried to embrace her but she shoved him away.

Trey said, "Get the fuck out of my house now."

Jessica said, "Motherfucker, you're one lucky ass man cuz I really want to go to the F.B.I. and tell them about all the coke you are bringing to Atlanta, but I don't want my son's father to be in jail."

Trey said, "Would you leave?"

Jessica said, "When are you gonna play catch with your son, Trey?"

Starr said, "This shit is too much for me to handle, Trey."

Trey yelled, "Mrs. Robinson, come and get your daughter!"

Jessica's mom appeared and said, "I told you. Let the courts handle him."

Trey said to Mrs. Robinson, "Can't you see she wants me?"

Jessica said, "I'm sorry Starr, I really am."

Trey planted another kiss on his son's face and said, "I'll come and pick you up soon, and we can play catch again."

Jessica grabbed T. J. and she, her mother, and T. J. exited the home.

• • •

When Shamari opened the door there were six U.S. marshals and four F.B.I. agents on his porch. He said, "Can I help you?"

One of the U.S. marshals, a redhead man said, "Looking for Shamari Brooks."

"Yeah that's me. Am I under arrest?"

The man said, "No, but I want you to come with me to answer some questions."

"Jada come here babe!" Shamari yelled.

When Jada arrived, she saw all the law enforcement and said, "What the hell is going on?"

The marshal said, "Good morning ma'am, we need to talk to your husband for a few hours."

Jada wanted to curse their asses out but the man was polite and she didn't want to cause any more commotion in the neighborhood. She was sure her nosey ass neighbors were somewhere with their curtains pulled back. Jada said, "Is he under arrest?"

"No."

"Well, he doesn't have to go then."

"Well, he can go now or we can pick him up later, after we get an order from the magistrate."

Shamari said, "Call my attorney Jada," He asked the marshal, "Where should I ask him to meet me?"

"The Federal Building downtown."

Shamari said, "Let me put on my shoes."

The man said, "Go ahead put your shoes on. And put a coat on too. It's kind of chilly out here."

Shamari got dressed and Jada phoned their attorney, Paul Gillium.

– PART TWO –

PART TWO

CHAPTER 12

STARR GATHERED A FEW OUTFITS FROM HER CLOSET. SHE WOULD STAY at her sister's house until she could get a place of her own. There was no way she could or would be in the house with Trey. He had fucked up bad, and she'd made up her mind it was best for her to leave. She gathered some socks and underwear and her pajamas. Trey burst in the room.

"Babe, I know you ain't gonna leave me because of this. Come on, babe, can't you see she's just jealous of our happiness?"

Starr folded her pajamas and put them in the Louis Vuitton overnight bag. She didn't respond to Trey.

"So now you're going to pretend you don't hear me?"

"What do you want me to say? I mean seriously, you have a child now. A child I didn't know about."

Trey sat on the edge of the bed and looked Starr in the face. His eyes were sad. He said, "I don't want you to go. Really, babe, don't leave me. I will do whatever it takes to be with you."

She put a pair of heels in her bag and said, "Trey, this shit really hurt me, dude. I don't know if I can get over this. I mean I thought you loved me."

Trey dropped to his knees said, "Baby, please don't leave me. I am nothing without you."

She tossed a pair of sneakers in her bag then folded her arms. "Trey, get off your knees. Ain't nobody got time for your bullshit."

"What are you talking about? I'm serious, babe. I don't want you to leave me."

"And what about Jessica and your child, NIGGA?"

He rose to his feet. "There is nothing I can do about T. J. He is here now. He was a mistake but I love my son, I'd be lying if I said I didn't love my son."

She picked up a new pair of shoes and slung both shoes at Trey's head barely missing him.

He said, "Okay you're mad because I love my son. What the fuck?"

A tear rolled down Starr's face before she began to sob, then she shouted, "You leave that baby out of this bullshit. He has nothing to do with this. You are supposed to love your son, but this is not fair. It's not fair that you betrayed me, and it's not fair that you kept this shit away from me all this time. This didn't just happen; you've known this shit for so many years. You are just fucking pathetic."

Trey said, "Jessica wants what you have. Can't you see that? She's just jealous of you,"

Starr said, "She is the one with the baby. Why would she want what I have? I want what she has."

Trey said, "You have me."

Starr said, "At this moment, I don't know if I want you. You're a goddamned liar, and you hurt me so much."

Trey stepped close to her and embraced her but she shoved him away. "Will you just get the fuck away from me!"

She sat on the bed and continued to sob. "The fucked up thing is that I want to believe you. I really do." She buried her face in her hands. "You've hurt me."

Trey sat beside her, patted her on the back and said, "I'm going to do whatever I got to do to make this right."

Starr said, "Trey, can you just leave me alone? Let me think."

He stood and left the room.

CHAPTER 13

ALL EYES WERE ON CRAIG AS HE DROVE UP TO THE VALET IN THE silver Maserati at the entrance of the W Hotel in Buckhead. He handed the key to the valet and hurried inside. Once inside he took the elevator to the 16th floor and walked to room 1623. Jada hugged him when he stepped inside. "What's up? Why couldn't you talk on the phone?"

He appeared genuinely concerned, but she still didn't know how much she should tell him. She said, "Have a seat."

He sat at a desk in the corner of the room. There were a couple of bottles of water on the table, with for sale tags placed on them by the hotel. He asked, "Do you mind if I drink one? I'll pay for it."

She said, "Drink it, don't worry."

He popped the top off the bottle and took a big swig. Then he said, "Please tell me what's going on."

She said, "The Feds picked up Shamari for questioning."

"Questioning? What did they charge him with?"

She paced before finally sitting on the edge of the bed and said, "I don't know why they picked him up. Don't know what they are charging him with." Although she felt that they'd picked him up because of what happened to Tony, she didn't want to say too much.

"They arrested him?"

"No," she said. Then she said, "I mean I don't think so."

He took another swallow of water and said, "I gotta hunch you're not telling me all you know. Listen I'm not a criminal, but I'm not the goddamned cops."

She sat still for a moment then wondered why in the hell had she called him in the first place. Why didn't she just call Lani? Somebody she knew would understand. She hadn't planned on explaining all of her business to the naive ass doctor.

He said, "Listen you don't have to tell me what's going on. The important thing is that you're safe."

When he said that, she realized why she'd called him in the first place. She didn't need him to solve her problems. She just wanted to know that she had someone. She didn't want to be alone. She smiled and said, "That meant more to me than you'll ever realize."

He said, "You need to leave him."

She heard him but ignored him.

He drank some more water. She grabbed the last bottle on the table, unscrewed the top and took a drink.

He said, "Look, I know I'm not your type, but this is getting dangerous."

Her eyes met his eyes and she said, "I spoke with his attorney, and he said that he'll be home soon."

He shrugged and said, "But surely this isn't the end. If the Feds are on to him, it's just a matter of time before they get him."

She said, "Why you gotta be so goddamned negative, Craig?"

He stood and laughed a little before saying, "I'm leaving, and you're fucking crazy. You are the one that called me over, and now I'm being negative."

He eased toward the door. He placed the empty bottle of water on the table and was about to turn to say goodbye when he saw that she was standing right behind him and their eyes met. He grabbed her head and kissed her before scooping her up and carrying her to the bed. He kicked off his converses, peeled her blouse off and admired her breasts. Goddamned he'd done a good job with them. She eased out of her skirt revealing a purple thong and her ass looked spectacular in it. He pulled the thong down with his teeth. Her clean shaved vagina made his erection throb, but his dick would have to wait, he would taste it first. Yummy.

• • •

Starr was at her sister Meeka's house, on the West Side of Atlanta, where she grew up right in the middle of the hood. Meeka was hood and so were her twin boys, DeVante and DeMontre. They were both seventeen years old and had dropped out of high school. Now they sold weed and pills out of Meeka's house. She pretended not to know what they were doing because they helped her out. The boys pretended to have a lawn service with no equipment and business was booming even in the middle of winter. Starr was trying to figure out why in the hell her sister needed help. Hell, she was on section 8 and she received over three hundred dollars worth of food stamps. But she wasn't there to ask questions. She just needed to get away from Trey. She sat in the den on one of Meeka's plastic covered sofas watching a reality show when Meeka walked in, blunt hanging from her mouth, wearing a skintight spandex body suit. "You need to get out of this house and get your mind off that nigga."

Starr looked up from the TV. "What you talking about?"

Meeka inhaled the blunt and passed it to Starr. She refused. "You know I don't smoke."

"No mo."

Starr said, "Huh?"

"Bitch, you don't smoke no-mo. Don't forget to say no-mo, you act like you ain't never smoked before."

"Ok, I don't smoke no-mo, you satisfied?"

A customer knocked on the door. A skinny black man with a dirty beard. Meeka said, "Twins are in the back room, Lenny."

Lenny said, "Hello, Miss Michaels." Lenny went to the backroom and minutes later, he left with a smile on his face, as he was leaving, a woman named Shatima came to stand on the porch. Meeka guided her to the twins' bedroom.

Starr was nervous about all this in and out and wondered how Meeka dealt with all the traffic.

Smiling, Meeka said, "One of twins' lawn care customers."

Starr said, "Of course."

Shatima entered the twins' room.

Meeka said, "You ain't no better than me cuz you got a dope boy giving you money and you moved out of the hood. Don't forget we come from the same place."

Starr took a deep breath. She didn't want to fight with her sister. She loved Meeka but she knew Meeka resented her because Meeka was envious of her and her lifestyle. Meeka was her older sister. Starr remembered when they were younger, all the dudes in the neighborhood wanted Meeka. She used to be amazing. She used to have this very tiny waist and an ass so perfect it looked like it had been sculpted. Guys would fight over her, then she got pregnant at seventeen by a loser named Kenny who was gunned down before the twins were born and Meeka was left to take care of her boys by herself and her life went downhill. She resented Starr because she was everything that Meeka was not.

"Look, Sis, I don't want to argue with you today."

"Why are you all uptight?" Meek puffed the blunt again. "You need to get out. Me and my girls, Cash and Tee, going to Onyx tonight. You need to come and get your mind off Trey."

"Naw, I'm just gonna chill."

Meeka said, "I don't see what the big deal is anyway. I mean the nigga fucked somebody else. I hope you didn't think that you were his only pussy. I mean any dude getting money is gonna have some side pussy. Point blank. Period." She laughed then said, "Hell, most of these clowns out here with less than five hundred dollars in their pockets are fucking too. Niggas are gonna do what niggas do. You know how the game go."

"He hid a kid from me, it's not that he cheated; it's that he kept a secret for years."

Meeka said, "Trey is a good dude, and he loves you."

Starr said, "I know he loves me, but this one is a hard one to get over."

Meeka said, "You better get over this shit real fast before somebody else is living in that goddamned mansion and pushing that Benz. These chicks out here is extra thirsty, I'm telling you."

Starr said, "I got my own money saved up. You know your little sister ain't stupid."

Meeka said, "How long you think that shit is gonna last?" She finished the blunt off. "You are used to a certain lifestyle now. You can't live over here with me."

Starr said, "Now that's where you're wrong. I like nice things, but they don't define me." Starr had prided herself on not letting material possessions blind her. She never thought anybody was beneath her. She never thought she was too good to speak to anybody and she never looked down on anybody.

"You want to live in the hood?"

Starr said, "I can, if I have to."

Meeka laughed and said, "Yeah, that'll be the day."

Starr said, "I'm here now ain't I? I could easily be at the Four-Seasons. I got money and I got credit cards."

Meeka said, "Well hell, since you got so much money, let me hold a couple of dollars, I want to buy a bottle at the club tonight."

Starr said, "Are you serious?"

"Dead serious. I wanna have some fun tonight and you should too."

"Naw I think I'm gonna stay in."

Another customer knocked on the door and Starr said, "On second thought, I think I'll go with you to the club." She didn't want to be there if the house got raided. She would find a hotel room in the morning.

CHAPTER 14

STARR ENTERED THE LOBBY OF THE W HOTEL WHEN SHE SPOTTED Jada with an attractive looking older white gentleman. Jada didn't see Starr. She figured this was the man Lani had been talking about at the Sushi restaurant. The married man. They headed outside. "What a skank." Starr thought. The couple eased out to the valet. She eased over to the window of the lobby, where she could see the happy couple waiting on the valet to bring the car. The man hopped into his silver Maserati and sped off. And Jada went back inside.

"Starr," Jada said as she approached the lobby.

Starr faced her and gave her a fake smile. "Hey, girl!" They hugged.

Jada said, "What you doing here?"

"Falling out with my dude, you know, had to get away for a while."

Jada said, "Go ahead check in. I'll be waiting here for you." She took a seat on a plush orange sofa. Starr joined her moments later.

"So why are you here?" Starr asked.

"Long story," Jada said.

"I got time," Starr said, not really wanting to tell her what was going on in her life. Buying time to decide what she would tell her about her life.

Jada didn't know Starr that well but she knew her man hustled as well, so she would understand her plight. She decided to open up. "The Feds came and got my boyfriend yesterday."

"What? I hate to hear that," Starr said. She'd met Jada's man once at Lani's birthday party. Light skinned dude, looked really tough. Not her type but drove a Bentley, so she assumed that he had money.

Jada said, "Yeah I know."

This chick had no morals. The man that had taken care of her was in jail, and here she was out at the W. Clearly just got done fucking some white dude. Starr was disturbed by this, but didn't let it show.

Starr said, "Does he have a bond?"

"Well, I spoke with his attorney before I checked in last night, and he said that they were going to have to let him go if they didn't charge him."

"So what happened exactly?" Starr wasn't trying to be nosey, but she always found stories of how dudes got busted interesting, because her man was in the same line of work. Whatever happened, she would have to make sure Trey avoided the same mistakes. Even if they didn't get back together, she loved him and didn't want him to get in any trouble.

"I really don't know. All I know is, he started hanging out with this dude that I had never seen until recently."

Starr said, "New niggas will do it every time." She stood, picked her overnight bag up and said, "I have to be heading to my room."

Jada said, "I'm about to call Shamari's attorney." She stood and said, "Maybe we should do lunch soon."

Starr said, "I would like that." She lied.

CHAPTER 15

"WHERE THE FUCK HAVE YOU BEEN?" SHAMARI ASKED WHEN JADA entered their home. He eyed her suspiciously.

"I checked into the W." She tried to kiss him, but he pushed her away.

"Ok, I get out of jail last night and you ain't nowhere to be fucking found," Shamari said. He paused before sitting on the leather sectional. "What kind of shit is that Jada?"

She sat on an armchair on the opposite side of the room.

"I had to get the fuck out of this house. I didn't feel safe in here."

"But why the fuck was your phone off? What if I needed you?"

She dug into her purse, retrieving her cell phone then presented it to him. "Look my phone is dead. I didn't have my charger with me." She took a deep breath and then said, "So you're out now, why all the drama?"

"That shit was real foul man, as much I do for you and you do me like this."

Jada sighed, "Look I'm sorry, what do you want me to say?"

Shamari said, "I guess you're right. I'm out now."

"What did you find out?"

"Well the phone that Tony used, he'd called me over 40 times in the last 4 days, when the Feds picked him up. They wanted to know who I was, and why was he calling me so much."

"How did they know that he called you, your phone is not in your name. Did he snitch?"

"My lawyer doesn't think so, doesn't mean that he won't say something later, but right now, I'm ok."

Jada said, "Why does he think you're okay?"

"Well they let me go; he said if they had anything, they wouldn't have let me go."

"But I don't get it? How did they know that he was calling your phone?"

"Because the dumb motherfucker had my name in his phone."

"Your full name?"

"Yeah, there was two Shamari's in his phone, and I was the one where he used the last name. Feds pulled my credit report and this is how they got me."

"What did you tell them? How did you get out?"

"I told them that I'd spoken with Tony. He said he really needed to talk to me. That was the reason he called me."

"Good thinking on your feet."

"Yeah I had to, man this shit is serious. Tony killed a federal informant and that's never good."

Jada said, "Why did you pay him to do this? This is bad. Real bad." She placed her phone back in her purse.

Shamari clutched a pillow and sighed. Then he stood, tossed the pillow back on the sectional and paced across the room before finally making eye contact with Jada. "You know Jada, This is something I never wanted to do. I never wanted to murder anybody or have anybody murdered, but the fact is people always betray me." He took a seat back on the sectional and said, "I did so much for that dude. I sent his son to private school. Paid for Don's mom's breast reconstruction after she had her breast removed and this is the thanks I get."

"What are you talking about?"

"Don betrayed me."

"You don't know that."

"I've been in this business long enough to know when something is not quite right. And something is not quite right, was not quite right with that dude, talking about how he didn't want to go to jail. Talking all this Christian bullshit." Shamari paused and said, "Well goddamn it, I don't want to go to jail either."

Jada said, "But now you've made things worse, baby. Things are worse than before. You realize that don't you?"

"I hate betrayal, I know I might go to jail for a long time. That's a fact but at least I can live with what I did. I did what I was supposed to do and that was to honor the game."

"The game? This is not a game, this is real life."

"I know it's real life, and if somebody trying to take my life, I have to do what I have to do."

Jada stood. "I have to charge my phone up." She eased toward the bedroom.

"Jada."

"Huh?"

"Don't ever betray me."

CHAPTER 16

STARR OPENED THE DOOR WHEN SHE HEARD THE LOUD KNOCK. SHE
thought it was room service but it was Trey. She attempted to close the
door but he wedged his foot in the door preventing that from happening.
"Can I get five minutes of your time Starr?"

"You need to leave. I'm gonna have the front desk call security."

"3 minutes."

She attempted to push the door, but Trey was too strong.

"1 minute."

She moved away from the door, and once he was inside, he said, "How
you been?"

"Trey, say what you gotta say. I ain't got time for this bullshit."

"Look, babe, I just came to apologize."

"You've already done that."

"You didn't accept."

She flopped on the bed and as he was about to take a seat next to her she
said, "Don't get comfortable in here. You are about to leave."

He smiled and at that moment she realized how much she missed her
man.

Trey said, "Look, babe, I miss you and I want you to come home."

She didn't say anything. She'd grabbed the remote control beside the
dresser and powered on the TV. Real Housewives of Atlanta was showing

Room service came and Starr signed for the club sandwich, potato
chips and diet coke then tipped the attendant 5 dollars. She returned

back to the bed with the tray in hand.

He said, "I fucked up big time. I know I did, but I'm here to make it right." He grabbed a chip from her plate.

She said, "How you gonna make this right, Trey? There is a goddamned kid and a baby mama. How the fuck am I supposed to deal with that?"

"So you've never made a mistake."

"Trey, I've always been faithful to you." She took a swig of her diet coke then bit into her sandwich.

Trey took a deep breath and said, "I try not to bring up the fact that you slept with O. G."

"I never slept with that man," Starr lied. She had slept with him a couple of times, when Trey was running the streets trying to make money and not giving her the attention she felt she deserved. O. G. was an older dude who had money, and he'd taken her shopping a couple of times. One of Trey's homies saw them out together and reported it back to Trey. Starr denied it, but Trey said his intuition told him something wasn't quite right. Starr never admitted to it because she didn't want to lose Trey.

"Look, Starr, you slept with O. G."

Starr said, "Okay, if I slept with him, what the fuck does that have to do with what's going on with you?"

He grabbed her hand. "Babe, nobody is perfect. Nobody."

"Trey, you hid a child from me for years. Why didn't you just tell me?"

Trey massaged Starr's hand and said, "Look I didn't want to lose the best thing I ever had. You complete me babe. When I'm with you, I don't see them other bitches, I only see you. We fit. It is just right and I like that. I know I'm not a perfect man, but I'm perfect for you."

Her pussy was getting moist. She'd never seen Trey being this sincere. She'd missed him so much. She missed his dick. She had to remind herself that she was mad at him.

"Listen, babe, my son is five years old, but I swear to you it's been only you for the last three years."

"Three years? What the hell?"

Trey said, "Well I'm being honest because I don't want to lose you."

"Trey you got more kids out there?"

"No, but I've fucked other chicks." He stood from the bed. "I'm just keeping it real."

"Why are you telling me this?"

"Cuz I don't want to lose you, and I felt so damn bad hiding T. J. from you. I don't want nothing to come up like this again."

"Are you saying you ain't gonna cheat?"

Trey said, "Like I said earlier, ain't nobody perfect, but I can promise you I'm gonna try my damn best not to go down that road again."

"So you don't know?"

"I haven't slept with nobody but you for the last three years and that's a fact."

She said, "Trey, I don't know about this man, I really don't."

Trey said, "What can I do to make it up to you? You name it, I'll buy it. I just want you home. What about that handbag I saw you looking at in Phipps Plaza? Or the watch that you asked me for? I'll go get all of that today. Just come home."

"Trey, you know I couldn't let you spend that kind of money on me. You know I'm not like that. I like nice things, yeah, but they don't define me. And I can't be bought; I'm not some low life ass gold-digger."

Trey said, "I know that, and that's what I love about you. You're one of the realest people I've ever met. Realer than most dudes in my circle."

She smiled, he was so sincere and so damn cute when he begged. He reminded her of a little boy, wanting something from his mother.

He said, "I swear to you, babe, I will not fuck up again."

"Trey, just give me a day or two to gather my thoughts."

Trey dropped to one knee and pulled a box out of his pocket. "Will you marry me?"

She covered her mouth. "Oh my God, Trey!"

"Open the box."

She said, "I don't want to."

"Please open the box; you don't have to accept, but hell you can at least look at the ring."

She opened the box and placed the sparkling six karat platinum diamond ring on her finger."

"You remembered my ring size."

"Come on, I know everything about you. Of course I remembered your ring size."

Starr said, "Trey, how much did this damn thing cost?"

"Don't worry about it?"

Starr said, "I know this ring is overpriced."

Trey said, "Keep the ring, babe. Don't worry about the cost of the ring. Can't put a price on love."

She stood and walked then looked in the mirror, glancing at the ring on her finger. "Damn this thing is amazing. I will get robbed for this."

She smiled again and then he smiled. He knew he was breaking her down. She said, "Trey, how much was this ring?" She removed it.

Trey said, "Eighty stacks."

Starr said, "Ain't no way in the hell I'm keeping this ring." She passed it back to him.

"You don't want it?"

"I can't be bought Trey. You know that about me and that's just too damn much for that ring, I would never wear something like that."

"Is it about the price?"

"No, it's about the motive. I mean were you really going to propose if you didn't fuck up?"

"Huh? You know we've talked about marriage and a family."

"I know we been talking about that shit for years. But it took you this long to make a move."

"Look, I'd been eyeing this ring for the last few weeks. You can ask Jesus, the gay dude in the jewelry store on Sixth Avenue."

Starr knew Jesus very well. Every time they'd visited New York she would buy little things from Jesus, but never anything amounting to over a couple of thousand dollars. She thought about phoning Jesus to verify Trey's story, but she believed him or at least she wanted to believe him. What girl didn't want to get married?

Trey attempted to pass her the ring back. She refused it and then said, "And another thing, we're going to have to stop acting like hustlers. I hate that shit. I mean nobody that I know can afford an eighty thousand dollar ring except hustlers. I don't like living like this Trey."

"I know, babe, but just bear with me, I'm going to go legit, I promise."

"I hope so cuz there is no way I'm marrying a drug dealer. I'm getting too old for this shit."

Trey smiled, "So you accept?"

"No, I didn't say all of that." She finished the rest of the chips, leaving a half-eaten club sandwich. She placed the tray outside the door.

Trey rose from the bed and embraced her and held her for a long time. Her heart beat next to his. She was where she belonged in the arms of her man. She'd missed him so damn much.

He released her from his grip and asked, "So when are you coming home?"

"I didn't say I was coming home."

"Look, Starr, I apologize that I have a kid. I apologize that I had the affair."

"Affair? I'm not your wife."

"You're my wife, we just don't have the papers yet, but you're my wife." She smiled.

Trey continued, "I even apologize that I'm a drug dealer, at this point in my life it's embarrassing, but one thing that's going to be hard to find out there is a real nigga, you might even find somebody with more money, but are you gonna find somebody more real?"

Starr said, "And I'm a real bitch."

Trey said, "I know, why do you think I'm fighting so hard? I need you to come back where you belong."

She opened the door and he stepped out into the hallway, still staring at her. His eyes on her breasts and her hips. He was more attracted to her now than the day they met. He was attracted to her soul.

He gave her a quick peck on the lips.

Starr said, "My ring budget is ten thousand and that's a lot."

He laughed, "Always the frugal one."

"No, I love nice things."

"Me too that's why I love you." He turned to walk away and she watched him as he got onto the elevator.

She closed the door and cried. Damn she wanted to go back home, but she wasn't quite over his betrayal. She called room service and ordered some more chips. She was stressed and junk food or sex was the only thing that was going to ease her mind and since her dick had gone, the potato chips would have to do.

CHAPTER 17

THE LUNCH CROWD HAD THINNED AT HOUSTON'S IN BUCKHEAD.
Black and Kyrie and a man named Rodriguez sat in the back of the restaurant in a booth. Kyrie and Rodriguez shared some nachos and Black nursed a Grey Goose and Coke. Nobody ordered food. Rodriguez was a tall man with an extra long face and thick eyebrows. Black sipped the vodka and said to Rodriguez, "So you know this dude?"

"Yeah I know him, but we're not like friends or nothing you know."

Black said, "How do you know him?"

Rodriguez said, "Wait a minute, why you wanna know all this?"

Kyrie said, "Answer the motherfuckin' question."

Rodriguez said, "Well there is a guy named E that live off Bankhead that sells weed, I sometimes cop from E."

Black said, "Wait a minute do you know E or Chris?"

Kyrie was chomping hard on those nachos dipping them in the salsa. He'd eaten about six when Black looked at him annoyed as hell.

Sensing Black was irritated he stopped and repeated what Black had just asked. "Do you know E or Chris?"

"I know both of them."

"So, E let you meet his connect?"

"Well I saw Chris one day at the gas station up the road from E's house and he gave me his number, and since I knew Chris was the source of the weed I figured he would give me a better ticket you know?" Rodriguez said. He scooped two chips up and ate them.

"So you do business with him?'

Rodriguez said, "What the fuck is this about? Do he owe you money or something."

Kyrie said, "No he don't owe us shit but you do motherfucker." Rodriguez was indebted to Black and Kyrie for some coke he'd been fronted years ago. Black would have normally had him fucked up but he'd not gotten around to it.

Rodriguez said, "Im'ma pay you, dude. As a matter of fact, I can give you a couple of thousand dollars today."

Black said, "No you're going to call your friend Chris and tell him you need a hundred pounds."

Rodriguez said, "Ok, give me the money. I think I can get it for around eight hundred a pound."

Black laughed and said, "Eight hundred dollars? I ain't paying no goddamned eight hundred dollars for shit. You understand me?"

"It's mid, man, this ain't no Reggie Miller. Homie, this is some good shit, nice green color, very little sticks in. It's straight fire. One thing I can say about this nigga is he keeps that good."

Black was irritated by Rodriguez singing Chris's praise, because not only was this motherfucker fucking his woman, it was clear to Black that he was *really* making money.

"What you wanna pay, I'll run it by him?" Rodriguez took a swig of water, then pulled out his cell phone scrolling through his address book looking for Chris's number.

Black said, "I ain't paying shit. You're going to call him and ask him for the hundred pounds and we're gonna take them from his punk ass. Black finished off his vodka and stared at Rodriguez—his black face forming the backdrop for pinkish eyes—intimidating Rodriguez.

"Come on, man, he ain't gonna ever believe no shit like that. The most I've ever gotten was twenty pounds."

"Call him."

"He doesn't talk on phones. I will text him."

Rodriguez texted Chris: *Yo' I need ten dime bitches for my partna's bachelor party. This was code 10 X 10 pounds of weed.*

Chris hit back: You ain't never wanted that many girls.

Rodriguez texted: Yeah I got a lot of people coming from South Carolina.

Chris: Okay will call you in a couple of hours to tell you where to meet me.

Rodriguez: *Cool.*

Black gave Kyrie a pound.

• • •

"Where are you going?" Shamari asked.

"Microdermabrasion appointment."

"Micro-what?"

"Making my skin smooth?" she said. She didn't feel like giving him a lengthy explanation about the procedure.

"How much you spending on that?"

Jada was startled that he asked her; he'd never asked her about money before.

Shamari said, "I'm just saying do you really need that shit? I mean you're turning into a surgery addict. You on that old Nikki Minaj shit. It's a waste of money." He said, "Well except for ..."

"The ass. You like the ass, but what about what I want and microdermabrasion is not a surgery."

"I mean facial, manis, pedis, you've had your boobs done. Not gonna count the ass, that one was my idea."

"So you gotta problem with what I wanna do now?"

"No, babe. I just gotta call from an attorney Tony hired. The guy said that Tony told him that I was going to pay him to represent him."

"How much is that going to cost."

"The retainer is $75,000, said it was so high because it was a possible capital murder case."

"Damn."

"I know right. Shit keeps getting worse and $75,000 is just the retainer; it's gonna probably end up costing twice as much."

"I gotta voucher for the microdermabrasion. The doctor gave it to me the last time I was at the office."

"He did?"

"Yeah, they like me over there."

"Well they should, all the goddamned money we have given them," he said.

"What's up with all the money comments? Are we getting low on money?"

Shamari said, "I'm just saying we've paid them a lot over the years, that's all."

"But you never answered the question."

He said, "Look, I've got something in the works."

She said, "But the money is low, right?"

He said," Yeah, it's getting a little low."

She said, "Am I gonna have to get a job?"

She annoyed him when she said things like that. He never wanted her money, but he'd never wanted her to be unemployed for a number of reasons. He knew that if he was ever unable to help himself, there was nothing she could do about it since she had no income.

"Hey I'm just saying you're an adult, and this shit is not gonna last forever."

CHAPTER 18

JESSICA STOOD ON THE PORCH WHEN TREY OPENED THE DOOR. "WHAT the fuck are you doing here?"

"Can I come in; I know she's not here."

"And how do you know that?"

"Saw her leave a couple of days ago and she hasn't returned."

"And how do you know all of that."

"Can I come in?"

He moved aside and let her inside and closed the door and said, "You fucking stalker."

"What?"

"Yes, you're a stalker."

"You think so. All I want is my son's father to spend time with him and I'm a goddamned stalker." She laughed. "All my friends told me all you black dudes are the fucking same, but no I didn't listen to them. I wanted to fuck with a bad boy. I wanted a drug dealer and this is what I got, a man that don't want to see his son."

"You know this ain't true. You know goddamned well this ain't true. I love my son."

"When are you gonna play catch with him then? That's all he ever says, my daddy is gonna play catch with me because he told me, but then you don't show up."

"You know this shit ain't about T. J. It's about you wanting me, and I don't wanna be with you."

"What the fuck does *Starr* have over me, and what kind of name is *Starr* anyway. This has to be the most ghetto name I've ever fuckin heard. Who names their kid *Starr?*"

"I knew this is what this was about!"

"Just because she has this huge ghetto ass, is that a reason to be with somebody? Because she don't work, she's gonna have you dealing drugs for the rest of your life or maybe spending the rest of your life in jail to keep up her ghetto fabulous lifestyle."

Trey said, "First of all, you don't know what the fuck you're talking about, and second of all, she does have a job."

"I hope you ain't still saying she does hair because that bitch is never at the salon."

"Jessica, what do you want from me? Just give me T. J. every other week and I will give you two thousand dollars a month. You know if we go to court, you ain't gonna get shit."

"Because you ain't earning shit legally."

"What the fuck do you want from me?"

"I want you to be with me and T. J. That's what I want."

"Listen I want to see my son, but I can't leave my girl to be with you. I love Starr."

Her mascara was now running. She didn't want to believe that he didn't want her. Why didn't he want her? She was more attractive and was educated and unlike Starr, she had a real job as an R.N.

Trey said, "You knew I was with her when we were fucking around. I told you that."

"But you liked me. You told me that too, remember?"

"Hey look, I was going through some things at the time. I'm sorry I told you that. I'm sorry we're going through this. I really am."

Jessica said, "Whatever." Sniffling through tears. He felt bad for her. He didn't like to see women cry.

She asked, "Do you have any tissue?"

He pointed to the bathroom.

CHAPTER 19

RODRIGUEZ ENTERED THE MODEST FULTON COUNTY HOME. IT WAS bare except for a sofa and a TV. It was cold inside. Typical drug stash house. They headed to the kitchen. Two duffle bags on the floor. Chris removed zip lock bags of marijuana and placed them on the table. The weed was lime green in color and the strong scent lit up the room.

Rodriguez picked up the weed, unzipped the baggie, and said, "This smells old and the color is too dark."

Chris said, "Nobody has said that but you."

Rodriguez said, "So how much you want for this?"

"We've already discussed prices. You know what my price is."

"But I'm buying so many this time and plus, this is not the best color."

Chris was getting angry. He knew he had a good product. He'd sold over a thousand in the last couple of days. Nobody else had said anything about the price of the weed. Nobody had anything to say about the color. He'd driven all the way from Peachtree City to make this transaction and now this nigga was acting like he wanted to renege.

Chris said, "Do you want the weed or not?"

Rodriguez exchanged text messages with somebody and then said, "Can we work on the price?"

Chris said, "The price is the price." Then they heard a thundering sound from the front door.

Goons kicked in the back door leading to the kitchen.

Chris ran to the drawer on the other side of the kitchen but by the time he opened the drawer to get his gun it was too late.

Three masked men stood in the kitchen. One of them placed a gun to the temple of Chris's head. "Where is the work, nigga?"

One of the other men told Rodriguez, "Get your bitch ass down before I blast you."

Rodriguez trying to play it off, "Please don't kill me, I have a son man, please don't hurt me." Then he emptied his pockets, dumping a small amount of cash on the floor. "I got more cash in the car, just don't shoot me."

"Motherfucker, shut the fuck up."

"Where the fuck is the work?" the other man asked Chris.

"That's all I got here."

"Where is the money?"

"Ain't no money here."

The man cocked the hammer of the gun. "I'm gonna ask you one more time. Where is the money?"

"There ain't no money."

He slapped Chris with the gun and fired it at the same time.

Chris said, "There's fifty grand upstairs in a suitcase in the bedroom in the back but that's all I got here."

They pistol-whipped Chris until he was unconscious. Blood oozed from his nose, both of his eyes were swollen from the impact of the pistol and his bottom tooth was knocked out.

The third man went upstairs and retrieved the suitcase. The three men left.

Rodriguez picked Chris up from the floor, staggered with him until he reached his car, then drove him to the hospital and told the emergency room receptionist that he was a stranger and had picked him up on side of the road.

CHAPTER 20

JADA MET CRAIG IN A GATED TOWNHOME COMMUNITY IN DUNWOODY.
It was a tri-level brick townhome with a two-car garage. Jada thought it was rather plain considering it had more security than the White House. Craig opened the door wearing a white robe with an unlit cigar dangling from his mouth. He kissed her and said, "I have a surprise for you."

"I love surprises."

With that stupid looking cigar hanging from his mouth he said, "I know you do, follow me."

He led her to a room that looked like a man cave with a leather sofa and a huge plasma TV. Two shopping bags rested on the sofa.

There were two shoe boxes inside the bag.

She opened the first box; there was a pair of heels, basic and cute. She opened the second box; there was a pair of peep toe wedges she saw Beyoncé wearing on one of the blogs. "Oh my God. How did you know?"

"I saw you looking at them on your tablet the day I visited your hotel room."

She eased out of her shoes and slid into the wedges.

"Where is your mirror?"

He directed her to a closet. "Open that closet. There's a full length mirror on the other side of the closet."

She pranced with her new shoes on, feeling like a princess. Not that she wasn't used to shoes. There had been times that Shamari would just hand her thousands of dollars and tell her to get what she wanted. But with all the drama going on, she hadn't been able to go shopping. She appreciated Craig treating her like a princess. She grinned and posed in the mirror.

He said, "Guess you don't like the first pair?"

"I love them, it's just I love the wedges."

"I can tell when you don't like something."

She said, "Hey I like them, what I don't like is that stupid cigar hanging from your mouth."

He frowned. "Not cool?"

She said, "Not cool at all, but you tried."

He removed the cigar and said, "I really don't smoke. I just like to pretend to look cool."

She said, "The hobbies of rich men."

He said, "Well since you didn't like the shoes, maybe you'll like this." He presented her a jewelry box.

She tore into it immediately and removed the diamond watch. She said, "Wow, this is amazing. You really didn't have to do this." She admired the sparkling watch.

She embraced Craig and said, "Thank you so much. You're so amazing."

"You deserve the best."

"Why did you have to be married?" She could really see herself falling for this man if the circumstances were right. She liked him a lot, but she still loved Shamari.

He said, "I don't believe you would be with me. Would you? You like the bad boys, the drug dealer lifestyle."

"Is that the reason for the silly cigar, were you trying to impress me? Trying to be a bad boy huh?"

He said, "Come on, I asked a question."

He'd called her out. She was drawn to bad boys. She like the thugs, not necessarily drug dealers, but she liked guys that would do whatever it took to get ahead, but she also liked power and Dr. Craig Matthews was a powerful man. "Answer the question."

"Look you're married, and there's no way of knowing what I would like if you weren't."

He said, "Let me give you a tour of the house."

She was very impressed with the house. He'd shown her the master bedroom with a huge walk-in closet. The two guest bedrooms. The kitchen was a chef style kitchen with expensive counters and cabinets. Finally he led her to the garage where his silver Maserati was parked beside a black one.

She said, "I didn't know you had two Maserati's."

He said, "Well I was hoping you'd be driving the other one by now."

"What are you talking about?"

"This could be yours."

"Yeah right."

"The townhome. Everything."

She said, "Everything has a price."

He grinned, "You know what I want?"

"You want to have your wife and me here as your personal fuck-toy."

His face became sad. "You know I don't look at you like that."

She said, "Dr. Craig Matthews, what would happen if you brought a black woman home."

He said, "Nothing."

"But you could never be with a black woman, only fuck a black woman."

He pressed his hands against her lips. "You know it's not like that."

She removed his hands. "How is it?"

"I love being around you. I love you."

He pulled her into him and accidently stepped on her new wedges. "You're going to ruin my new shoes."

"And I'll buy you more. I'll buy you whatever you want."

He kissed her, then unbuttoned her bra. Her huge implants spilling out. He put his mouth on them, sucking them like an animal. She kicked the wedges off. His hand was now on her perfect little ass.

He pulled her pants down, revealing a yellow G-string contrasting perfectly against her black skin. His dick jumped out of the white robe and she grabbed it with her hand then she dropped to her knees and took him in her mouth.

"Oh my fuckin God!" he yelled. She was glad she was satisfying him, but him yelling "Oh my fuckin God" was corny as hell and it was something a black man would never say. She played with his balls and he said, "Stop, stop, this feels too good to be true."

She stood and they kissed again.

He threw her on the hood of the Black Maserati (the one that would be hers) and ripped her G-string off. He dropped his robe. His dick still rock solid. She was now lying on her stomach. When he entered her, she came fast. Not because he was so wonderful, but it was something about having sex on such an expensive car that turned her on. She wished the engine was running.

CHAPTER 21

LANI WAS DRIVING LIKE A NASCAR DRIVER TO THE HOSPITAL WHEN she got a call from Black.

"Hello."

"Hey, Babe."

"Black, I ain't got time for this shit today."

"What's wrong?"

"My man's in the hospital."

"What happened?"

"I don't know, I think he got robbed."

"Damn, yeah? Niggas is real thirsty out here now. I'm sorry to hear that."

"Yeah, so I'm gonna have to talk to you some other time."

Black said, "So you want me to meet you at the hospital?"

Lani said, "Black, you gotta be out of your fucking mind."

"What? I'm just saying you need somebody to help you get through this, and what better person than me."

"I ain't got time for your bullshit. You know my man would not approve of shit like that."

"He's unconscious, how is he gonna know."

"What the fuck do you mean, he's unconscious. I ain't tell you no shit like that."

"If he got shot then he's probably doped up."

"I don't know what happened."

"Okay, go handle your business. Call me when you're done okay."

She hung up the phone and phoned Chris's brother Michael who was already at the hospital. "I'll be there in fifteen minutes."

Michael said, "Okay he's in ICU."

Lani prayed that Chris would be okay. He was such a good man, she was happy God had sent someone like him into her life after such a roller coaster relationship with Black. Chris was like a breath of fresh-air. He was the opposite of the very loud and flamboyant Black, but he was no sucker and he was street smart. She wondered how he'd gotten robbed. Who was responsible for it and how he'd let his guard down. When she entered the hospital, she signed in at the nurses' station and headed to ICU.

Lani started weeping as soon as she saw Chris with all the IV's hooked up to him. His eye and lips were swollen and he was unconscious.

Michael said, "It's real bad, Lani." They embraced.

"What do you know about this, Michael?"

"I don't know shit! All I know is whoever did my brother like this is gonna fuckin' die." Michael was usually calm and Chris was the wild one. Lani had never seen this side of Michael before.

"Chris don't fuck with shady characters. How did this happen?"

Lani said, "I don't know." This just didn't make sense to her. She knew that Chris almost never went outside of his circle. He'd told her more than once that he only had four customers and he'd known all four of them for years. What could have happened? Did Chris go outside of his circle? There was no way of knowing.

A doctor came in, a thin Asian man with speckled glasses, who introduced himself as Dr. Wu. He said, "Lani? Are you Mr. Jones's wife?"

"No I'm his girlfriend."

"He's in a coma right now. He's suffered severe brain trauma."

Lani said, "How long does comas usually last?"

"It could be a day, could be a week, could be years, ma'am. It's hard to tell right now."

Michael held her hand and Lani said to the doctor, "So what else are you going to do?"

He said, "There's not much we can do right now. The good news is the internal bleeding has stopped and that's a good sign."

Lani said, "But we don't know when he's going to come out of the coma?"

Dr. Wu said, "We don't know, but just keep the faith, I've been a doctor for twenty-five years and I can tell you having faith does help in these situations."

Lani said, "I've started praying already."

When Dr. Wu left the room, a tall gorgeous brown-skinned woman with a very expensive weave entered the room.

Michael said, "Cassie." He embraced the woman and then said, "He's not doing good at all."

Cassie eyed Lani, finally Michael said, "Cassie, this is Lani."

The women exchanged fake smiles and Cassie said, "I'm Michael and Chris's cousin from Connecticut."

Lani said, "Pleased to meet you. Chris has never said anything about family in Connecticut."

Michael said, "Yeah, we have lots of family in Connecticut."

Cassie said, "I live in Atlanta now, in the Sandy Springs area."

Lani said, "Oh okay."

Cassie said, "What happened?"

Lani said, "There is no way of knowing right now, Chris is in a coma. He got beaten up really bad, but how it happened is a mystery. Thank God he's still living."

Cassie said, "Yes, I don't know what I would do without Chris."

A thin blond nurse name Barbara entered the room and passed Michael a zip-lock bag containing just over three hundred dollars in cash, a wallet and his cell phone . "These items were found in his pocket."

Michael said, "Thanks."

When the nurse left the room, Michael said to Lani, "I'm going to go home now." He removed the wallet and the money and passed it to her. "I'm going to hold on to the phone till tomorrow. I got a feeling this phone has some clues to what might have happened."

Lani hugged Michael.

Cassie said, "I'm gonna leave now too." She shook Lani's hand.

CHAPTER 22

STARR WAS HAPPY TO BE BACK IN HER HOME AND TREY WAS EVEN happier that she was back where she belonged. He couldn't stop kissing her. He grabbed her bags and carried them to the bedroom. She followed, hopped up on her canopy bed and grabbed the remote control and turned the television on.

He kicked off his shoes, fell right next to her and kissed her on the cheek. "So glad you're home."

"I'm glad to be here, I don't like hotels, and I damn sure don't like being in the hood with my sisters and my two thug ass nephews.

"Yeah, when I went over to find out where you were, one of those little niggas asked me to give him some work. I'm like dude you know I can't do that."

Starr said, "I don't know why not, they're getting it from somebody."

Trey laughed. "That's what he said. His exact words were 'Uncle Trey Im'ma get mine from somebody, we might as well keep it in the family'."

Starr shook her head. "Those little bastards and my goddamned sister think nobody knows what is going on, trying to pretend that she don't know what's going on."

Trey said, "Well that's exactly how I was when I was their age. Started hustling in the hood, asking the older boys to give me work, but never out of my mama's house."

Starr said, "That is so trifling."

Trey said, "Hopefully they don't get caught."

Starr said, "I would hate that to happen to my sister."

He planted more kisses on her cheek. She hated to admit that she was happy to be with him.

The doorbell rang and he stood and headed to the door. She walked behind him, wondering who was at the door. He opened the door and there was a box on the step. The UPS man drove away.

Starr said, "What's in the box?"

"Just a few things I ordered for T. J. from Zappos."

"So when is me and Mr. T. J. gonna get acquainted?"

"Soon."

Starr said, "I hope so" and disappeared into the bathroom. A few moments later she came holding a long blond stand of hair. "Trey what the hell is going on? Why is this in my bathroom? You had that bitch here didn't you?"

Trey just stood there looking dumb wondering what he was going to say. It was obvious Jessica had been there. How was he going to explain this without looking guilty? He said, "Babe, Jessica was here but nothing happened."

Starr said, "You expect me to believe that shit?" She headed to the bedroom and gathered her things and walked toward the door before he blocked her path.

CHAPTER 23

SHAMARI SAID, "HEY, WHEN DID YOU BUY THIS WATCH?" HE HELD UP the Cartier, admiring the sparkling diamonds.

"What are you doing with my things?"

"First of all, we live together, so your things are my things. Secondly I was looking for the extra key to my truck that I'd put in your drawer months ago."

"Whatever."

"Why are you getting so defensive over something that I paid for?"

Jada didn't know how to answer him. It was clear that he thought he had bought the watch.

She said, "Not defensive, I asked you a question."

He said, "But I asked you a question first."

"I've had this watch for a long time."

"Really?"

"Yes, really. I brought this watch over a year ago."

"Why haven't I seen it?"

"I don't know. Maybe if you paid more attention to me, you would notice things.

He said, "That watch looks like it cost about 20 grand at least."

"Something like that."

"How much did the watch cost?"

"What difference does it make?"

"He said, "Bitch, it makes a lot of difference, and let me remind you, it's my money you spent on this."

She said, "So if you give me money, it's still yours?"

"Jada, how much did the damn watch cost?"

"I've never heard you want to know how much something cost. Is there something you want to tell me?"

He looked away, but didn't answer her.

"Shamari, why are you tripping about this watch?"

"I haven't seen the watch, that's all."

"There are a lot of things you haven't seen, I've never seen you act like this about the cost of something."

He said, "I just gotta watch my money that's all."

She said, "What is that supposed to mean?"

"What do you think it supposed to mean?"

"Question with a question," she said and took the watch from him.

He said, "Listen the money is getting a little low."

"How did that happen?"

He sat in a chair that is in the corner of the bedroom. "Well before Don got indicted, I'd given him four kilos. I don't know if the Feds got them or not, but he told me they'd gotten the drugs when they picked him up. Then I paid Tony for the job. And then paid for his attorney, not to mention I bought 16 keys that was absolutely garbage, I've lost about 400,000 in the last month."

"So how much do you have?"

"Maybe about fifty grand."

"Maybe?"

"Well I don't know yet."

"So we're broke?"

"Basically."

"Do you want me to sell the watch?" she asked, though Craig had given her the watch, she'd been with Shamari for years. He'd looked out for her and her family so many times. She would gladly sell the watch.

He said, "Not yet."

"But we're broke," she said.

He said, "Damn near."

She tried to hand him the watch. He refused it and she was glad. This was not what she signed up for. She wanted to leave him. Not because he was broke but because she was pretty sure the Feds were on his ass, but if she left him now everybody would swear it was because he didn't have as much money as he'd had before. Damn.

• • •

Lani sat by Chris's bedside when Michael called. "Mike, what's up?" she asked.

"Do you know who Rodriguez is?"

"No. Why?"

"He was the last person who Chris texted. He'd given him directions to a home. I think this dude knows exactly what the fuck happened to my brother, and I intend to get to the bottom of this shit."

"But you don't know him, how are you gonna find out what happened?"

"The streets talk, and if I find out this motherfucker had something to do with my brother getting hurt—"

"Mike" Lani cut him off. She didn't want him to say too much over the phone.

"Seriously, Lani, somebody is gonna get hurt."

"I understand but careful what you say."

Mike was breathing hard on the phone, barely able to contain himself. He said, "Any changes in bruh's condition?"

Lani glanced over at Chris. His eyes still shut and sleeping like a baby. She loved him and she wanted him to get well. She wanted to find out what happened to him just as bad as Mike did, but she didn't want Mike to get in trouble. God, that's the last thing their parents would need, one son in jail and the other in the hospital.

Lani said, "No change. When are you coming back to the hospital?" She wanted to calm him down.

"No time soon, my first order of business is to find out where the fuck Rodriguez is. Somebody has to pay for this."

CHAPTER 24

TREY SAID, "YOU AIN'T GOING NO FUCKING WHERE." HE STOOD IN front of Starr and she was trying to push him out of her way.

"Trey, move before I call the police on your ass. I know you don't want that."

He said, "Listen, Starr. Jessica was here. She popped up when you weren't here. Gave me that bullshit that we needed to be together and I dismissed her ass."

"Yeah you dismissed her right after you fucked her." She pushed Trey. His muscles were rock solid and he wasn't moving. She couldn't move him.

"I didn't fuck nobody. She used the bathroom."

"And the bitch put her hair in the sink? Yeah right, Trey." She pounded his arm. Still unable to move him.

"I didn't have sex with that woman. I swear to you."

Starr said, "Well did it ever occur to you that you should have called me, or at least told me she'd been over here?"

"Starr, goddamn it, it slipped my mind, I didn't think it was an issue."

"Your baby's mama at our home while I'm not here, and you think it's not an issue. Come on, Trey, do you think that I think you're that fucking stupid?"

He stepped aside and she didn't attempt to walk by him. He stared at her knowing she was furious. Wondering what she was going to do next. He didn't want her to leave. He had to convince her to stay.

Starr said, "Trey, you're a grown ass man. Older than me. How many times am I going to have to forgive your silly ass?"

"Babe, it's not like I made a mistake."

She shook her head. "Another mistake, should I expect another kid to pop up?"

"Cut it out, you're being stupid now."

"Am I?"

"Insecure as hell."

"First of all, I ain't insecure about shit. I trusted you."

"I know and I fucked up, but if you're gonna keep holding that shit over my head, you can go."

Starr said, "It's that easy huh. That easy to kick the goddamned woman that you just proposed to out."

Trey said, "Ain't shit about this easy. It's just that I can't take being accused of some shit that I didn't do."

"I told you she came over talking about how we need to be one big happy family. I told her ass to take a hike."

"Real talk?"

"Real talk." He kissed her forehead then pulled her into him. They locked lips and he scooped her up and took her back to the bed. He removed her blouse as she pulled down her jeans revealing a pair of pink boys shorts that bear hugged her ass and lifted it. She peeled her bra off revealing small but suckable tits. He loved them. He kissed her neck before dropping his jeans. His cock standing at attention.

She gripped his penis then and whispered, "I missed him."

"What about his owner?"

"Of course I missed you, babe."

"I don't want you to ever leave me again."

"Don't ever give me a reason to leave."

"I love you."

"I love you too." She kissed him again and between breaths she asked. "Are we still getting married?"

He said, "Have I ever lied to you?"

She gave him a funny look and then said, "Actually no, but you damn sure withheld some information."

They laughed. Then she took his manhood deep into her mouth. He stood her up and pushed her on the bed and said, "I want to pleasure you. I owe you."

She was lying on her back and he dove between her legs. He sucked and licked her clit until she screamed, "Put it in me please!"

He sucked her clit vigorously and she continued to scream. He placed a finger inside her then switched alternate fingers until she had multiple orgasms. He stood and walked over to the window. He dropped the blinds to make it completely dark. His penis still standing at attention. She lay on the bed in a fetal position trembling, very much satisfied. He positioned her until she was lying on her back then he entered her. She yelled, "Goddamn, nigga, you're an animal!"

He grinned then kissed her and she bit his neck hard while clawing his back. She loved feeling his bulging muscles. He was so big and he made her feel so safe. She felt like a little girl and he was her protector. The feeling was turning her on. He flipped her over on her stomach and entered her from behind, slapping her ass. "Goddamn it, you know I love that shit!"

"Call me daddy."

"Daddy."

She really didn't like calling him daddy. In fact she hated that shit but it seemed to turn him on and she wanted him to be satisfied too.

He said, "I love you so much."

Tears trickled down her face. She loved him too and there was no place she would rather be.

She came two more times before he finally exploded and wiped his cum all over her big beautiful ass.

- PART THREE -

CHAPTER 25

LANI MET STARR AND JADA AT THE BAR IN THE W ON 16TH STREET.
They sat in a comfortable little sectional in the corner. Jada and Starr
had a martini while Lani nursed a Long Island Ice tea. Starr remembered
the last time she was at the hotel, a couple of days ago, when she had
seen Jada with the white dude. She was reminded of just how scandalous
this chick was. She tried not to think about it, but she knew she had to
keep an eye on Jada. She was the type of bitch that would sleep with your
man if given the chance.

Lani said, "I'm so glad you convinced me to come out, I was really
feeling guilty about going out having fun while my man is in that damn
hospital."

Starr said, "You need to be out. You've been in that hospital for three
days straight."

Lani said, "I just feel so guilty about me out here having fun while he's
basically fucked up." She started to tear up. "Somebody beat my baby bad."

Jada placed her hand on Lani's knee and said, "Starr is right. You can't
live your life in this hospital. Chris would understand."

Starr was sure that if Jada's man was in the position Chris was in, that
she would be out partying, doing all the things that she had done before.
Starr was convinced she was not a good woman."

Jada said, "Don't beat yourself up. You know this is the game. You gotta
take the good with the bad and pray and keep your faith in God. He will
work it out."

Starr said, "Chris is a good man. God will work it out."

Lani said, "I'm sure he will."

Starr turned to Jada. "Is everything okay with Shamari? Did he ever get out?"

Lani said, "Out? Where has he been?"

Jada felt bad that she hadn't spoken with Lani, but she had so much going on the past few days she didn't have a chance to speak to her about Shamari.

"Shamari got picked up by the Feds, but he's out."

Lani gave her the side eye.

"Hey he didn't get charged," she found herself saying. Knowing that him getting out of jail sounded strange to them. Nobody got out of jail once the Feds picked them up unless they talked.

Lani said, "What happened?"

"Shamari's friend Tony murdered somebody and they just wanted to know if he knew anything about it. Tony told the Feds that he didn't so they let Shamari go."

Starr said, "Thank God. Nobody wants to be down for a murder."

Lani said, "Yeah but sometimes you gotta do what you gotta do." Thinking about the person who hurt her baby.

Starr turned to Jada and said, "What's up with you and the white dude?"

Jada said, "What white dude?"

"The one I saw you with in this lobby the other day?"

Jada bristled, thinking about the nerve of this bitch trying to put her on blast. If she'd wanted to know about the white dude, why didn't she ask the other day?

Jada said, "He's just a friend."

"Really? Looks like it was more than a friend to me."

Lani said, "Who is she talking about? Dr. Handsome?"

Jada said, "Yeah, we met here the other day for drinks."

Starr said, "While your man was in jail."

Jada said, "Why the fuck are you all up in my business, bitch?"

Starr said, "Cuz that was some trifling ass shit, I just don't appreciate trifling bitches."

Jada stood up and slid her shoes off. She was used to bitches coming at her like that because she looked like a Barbie Doll, but she could fight like a dude. Growing up in the projects she had to fight every day.

Starr said, "You don't wanna go there, trust me."

Jada said, "Bitch, trust me!"

Starr said, "Nobody can trust your ass, not even the man you claim you love." Starr was upset when she thought about Jessica and how she'd been sleeping with Craig. Jada was the kind of chick that would play the side bitch role gladly, and she didn't like women like that.

Lani said, "You know y'all are my two best friends. Please both of y'all have a seat."

Jada said, "I just ain't gonna stand here and let somebody disrespect me."

Starr said, "But you disrespecting ya man. A nigga that's out here hustling so you can wear designer shit; so you can drive foreign cars. Trust me when you fuck that up, it's over."

"Whatever, bitch."

"You can think that white man wants you if you want to. That white man don't want nothing from you but ass. Believe that. You're nothing but ass to him."

Lani put her hands over Starr's mouth. "Will you just stop it!"

Jada was about to say something and Lani said, "My man is in the hospital fighting for his life. Can you just shut the fuck up!"

Jada sat back down and finished her martini off without saying a word. Damn she wanted to give Starr a beat down. Staring down at the watch that Dr. Craig Matthews had bought her. Was she nothing but ass to him?

CHAPTER 26

WHEN LANI ENTERED THE HOSPITAL ROOM, CHRIS WAS SITTING UP IN the bed, alert flicking back and forth between Sports Center and the NFL network. Lani ran over and hugged him. "Baby you're ok!"

The nurse entered the room and said, "Yeah, came to a couple of hours ago. We tried to call you on your cell, but it kept going to voice mail."

Chris smiled at Lani and they made eye contact and they kissed.

Chris said, "I still don't remember what happened."

The nurse said, "His short term memory is gone."

"No!"

When the nurse left the room Lani said, "You got robbed, baby. Somebody beat you up and robbed you. Dropped you off at the hospital."

"Really?"

"Yeah."

"Why?"

She looked at him and wondered how much of his memory had been affected. How could she explain why he'd gotten robbed?

He said, "Look I know I'm a hustler, so you don't have to look at me strange. My memory ain't that shot, I was just wondering why would somebody rob me?"

She laughed at him and said, "That's what Michael wants to know. He thinks some dude named Rodriguez had something do with it."

"Bitch assed Rodriguez?"

"I don't know him."

"He's a real bitch, trust me, and if I find out he had something do with this, he's gonna be dealt with."

His cousin, Cassie, entered the room and she and Lani exchanged pleasantries.

Lani said, "Why didn't you tell me about your gorgeous cousin?"

Chris said, "I've told you about Cass before."

"I don't remember."

"I told you about my cousin that went to Spelman."

Lani said, "Yeah, but you were so vague about it, just saying that you had a cousin that went there."

Cassie said, "Men are always vague." She passed Chris the soda and kissed him on the cheek.

The kiss made Lani a little uneasy, but she was his cousin. But damn they were grown. Did grown cousin's kiss?

Lani said, "So how are y'all related?"

Chris said, "My daddy and her mom are brother and sister."

Lani said, "Oh okay."

Chris said, "Her mother made sure me and Mike knew Dad's side of the family after he passed when I was eight years old."

Lani said, "That was nice of her."

Chris said, "I want to get the hell out of here."

Cassie said, "The nurse said they're going to keep you at least till in the morning. Waiting on some test to come back."

Chris said, "No hell they ain't! I'm leaving here tonight."

Cassie shrugged.

Lani said, "You know your cousin, if he says he's gonna leave tonight, you better believe he's leaving tonight."

Cassie said, "Unfortunately."

CHAPTER 27

TWO MEXICANS SAT IN THE LIVING ROOM WITH SHAMARI, WHEN JADA arrived home. Shamari kissed Jada on the cheek. Jada stared at the Mexicans wondering why they were there, but she didn't bother to ask. One was short and dumpy and looked as if his meals consisted of mostly bean burritos and the other one was kind of tall and looked almost like a white man. The tall one spoke, but the short and dumpy one didn't. Jada excused herself. When she was in the other room, she eavesdropped on the conversation.

Shamari said, "If I could pay for it, I would."

Dumpy said, "Amigo, give me some collateral, and I will give you what you want."

Shamari said, "I ain't got no collateral, if I had collateral I wouldn't be asking you for shit."

Tall guy sounded like he'd been born in the U.S., barely any accent at all. He said, "Shamari, you already owe us 200 thousand dollars. There is no way in hell I can give you 10 kilos without getting anything up front."

"I've been dealing with you for eight years, you know I'm good for it."

Dumpy said, "You need to adjust your lifestyle man. You're creating these bills."

Shamari said, "Don't tell me what the fuck to do with my money." He stood and paced and then said, "I can give you my Cadillac Escalade, it's paid for."

Tall guy laughed. "You want a hundred thousand dollars' worth of product for a sixty thousand dollar car that we can't get sixty for?"

Shamari said, "Look, Fred, I've never asked you for anything. I've never owed you nothing. You gotta look out for me and I promise you, I'll pay you man."

"How much money do you have?"

"I've got about 20 grand."

"And the car?" Fred asked.

"Yeah."

Fred took a deep breath and then said, "Keep the car, give me the money and I'll give you the work."

Shamari said, "You won't regret it."

"I hope not, for your sake bruh." Fred stood and he and Shamari made eye contact and he said, "If you don't pay me, they're coming for you."

Shamari said, "I know."

Fred said, "One question? How did this happen?"

Shamari said, "How did what happen?"

"How the fuck did you go from spending a million dollars a month with me to having only twenty grand?"

Shamari said, "I don't know man."

Fred said, "You black dudes always like to shine. Always trying to impress motherfuckers and not have any money. Never shine until you got at least a million dollars."

Shamari said, "Dude, I've had money before."

Fred said, "But you don't now."

Shamari didn't respond. He wanted to though. He'd known Fred for over five years. Delivered him millions of dollars and now he was being talked to like a child.

Fred said, "I'm gonna deliver the work tomorrow, you just better have the money."

Shamari said, "I'm good for it. Don't worry."

CHAPTER 28

IT WAS 4:30 IN THE MORNING WHEN TREY GOT A CALL FROM THE Harris County jail. He pressed six to accept.

"Trey, it's Monte, can you get in touch with my mama and tell her they arrested me?"

Trey couldn't believe what he was hearing. Monte was a driver. The one he'd hired to bring the drugs back to North Carolina. Tell mama he'd been locked up was the code that he'd been busted with the work. There was no need to say anything else over the phone. Trey would have to hire him an attorney and get him out on bond. How did this happen Trey wondered. His method had been air-tight. Who could have snitched? He had to call Kenny, his Houston connect, to let him know what had happened. Tell him to trash his phones.

"Where are you?"

"Harris County jail. Houston."

"What if she asks about a bond?"

"Tell her I don't have one yet. Just need an attorney."

Trey said, "I'll call her now." He hung up the phone; there was no need to talk to him any further. Monte had picked up forty kilos of coke. Trey didn't know what was more disappointing, his friend getting locked up or the fact the he'd lost four hundred thousand dollars.

He called his attorney, Dr. Anderson Rozelle. His lawyer was both a doctor and an attorney. Dr. Rozelle picked up on the third ring. "Trey, what's wrong?"

"A childhood buddy of mine got busted in Houston with a shitload of drugs."

"Texas?"

"Yes."

"I don't practice law in Texas but I got a couple of friends down there. Does he have a bond?"

"No. We need to get him one."

"What's his record like?"

"Doesn't have one as far as I know."

"I'm gonna look into it."

"Can you find out what happened?"

"Give me till three o'clock. I will call you back and let you know what I found out. Meanwhile don't talk to this guy at all. If he calls you back, don't answer the phone."

Trey laughed and said, "I'm not worried about him. This is like my brother."

"Trey, sons put mothers in jail. Don't ever forget that."

"Yeah you're right."

"Trey, before I forget, what is your friend's name?"

Trey chuckled and said, "I guess that would help you out, right? His name is Monte, Monte Rogers, age 32."

Trey hung up the phone. Dr. Rozelle was right. He lay in the bed. Starr still sound asleep. He stared at the ceiling and wondered how in the hell did his organization get infiltrated. Who could have snitched?

CHAPTER 29

IT WAS 10:30 IN THE MORNING IN A SUBURB IN SOUTH-EAST ATLANTA
when Rodriguez came out of his one bedroom apartment holding a bacon
and egg sandwich wrapped in a paper towel. He was on his third bite
when Michael smacked the shit out of him. Rodriguez coughed up egg.

Michael grabbed him around his neck.

Rodriguez dropped his sandwich. His size ten Nikes now covered in
eggs.

Chris said, "Motherfucker, you know what this is about."

Stunned Rodriguez stared Chris in the face. How did he recover from
the brutal beating so fast? When did he get out of the hospital? "Please,
Chris, don't hurt me."

Chris put a gun to Rodriguez's ribs and said, "Open the door motherfucker.
Let's go in your apartment and sit down for a while."

Rodriguez trembled as he attempted to place the key in the hole. Once
inside they all sat in the living room area. This room was bare except for
a sectional and a plasma TV.

Chris pointed the gun at Rodriguez temple and said, "So are you gonna
tell me what the fuck happened? Who made you rob me?"

"What do you mean tell you what happened?"

Michael slapped the shit out of Rodriguez again and said, "Next time
it's gonna be with my motherfucking gun if you don't tell me what
happened to my brother."

Rodriguez said, "Niggas bust in and robbed us. You know what happened."

Chris said, "I don't remember shit, but I do know you had something to do with it because you were the last motherfucker I talked to."

Michael said, "Strip motherfucker I want you to get butt motherfucking naked."

Rodriguez said, "Are you serious?"

Chris shot Rodriguez in the foot making him howl.

Michael said, "Strip, bitch."

Rodriquez peeled out of his clothes, trying to balance himself on one foot. Now standing up in his tighty-whiteys covered in skid marks.

Chris said, "Nigga, you don't know how to clean your ass."

Michael said, "Come out of those dirty ass drawers too."

Rodriguez trying to nurse his bleeding foot, kicked his tighty-whiteys to the other side of the room.

Michael presented an extension cord. "So you gonna tell us what happened?"

"We got robbed."

Michael lashed Rodriguez across his ass with the extension cord. "Tell me what the fuck happened, now, nigga."

He lashed him again and Chris shot his other foot. Rodriguez was now lying on the floor. Both feet bleeding. "What the hell happened, nigga?"

Rodriguez yelled "Please don't shoot me again! I'm going to tell you."

"Tell me then, or I'm blasting your ass."

"Kyrie told me to set you up."

"What the fuck do you mean, 'Kyrie told you to set me up'? Who is Kyrie?"

"My cousin!"

"So you been talking to your cousin about me?"

"No he asked me did I know you."

"Where does your cousin live?" Chris said.

"I can't tell you that."

Chris fired a shot into Rodriguez's left ass cheek and he howled again.

Chris went to the kitchen, got a paper towel and used it to scoop the shitty underwear that Rodriguez had kicked in the corner. Chris then stuffed them in Rodriguez's mouth. He was gagging for air before Chris finally pulled the underwear out of Rodriguez's mouth.

"You gonna tell me about your cousin or else."

"Well it was Black's idea!"

"Black?"

"Black is Kyrie's friend"

"Kyrie got a mohawk?"

"Yeah."

Michael asked, "You know these clowns?"

"I do?"

"From where?"

"Well Black is Lani's ex."

"The nigga you fought at the basketball game?"

"Yup."

"Where does Black live?" Chris asked.

"I don't really know Black." Rodriguez said.

Chris grabbed the underwear and put the skid mark right up to his nose.

"I don't know!"

"Well you're going to have to show us where your cousin live or I'm firing at your ass again and stuffing your mouth with your shitty ass drawers and duct taping it shut."

"He has an apartment off Old National."

"Where off Old National?"

"I don't know the name of it, but I can show you."

Michael said, "Okay motherfucker show us."

Rodriguez attempted to stand but he fell. "Man I can't walk," he said with blood oozing out of both feet and his ass cheek.

Chris threw him his clothes. "Put these on."

Rodriguez managed to muster up enough strength to put his clothes on. Chris and Michael carried him to the car without being noticed by neighbors. Rodriguez pointed out his cousin's apartment. Chris and Michael dropped him off in front of the same hospital where he'd left Chris days earlier. His mouth taped shut and those skidded underwear taped on his forehead.

CHAPTER 30

DR. ROZELLE CALLED TREY, WHO ANSWERED ON THE SECOND RING.
"What did you find out?"

"Your friend is still being held without a bond."

"That's not good."

"Not at all, but the good news is Monte hasn't made a statement."

"How do you know?"

"I have my ways of knowing."

"We gotta get him out of there."

"Yeah. I have a friend down there. A very successful trial lawyer named Thomas Matlock."

"Matlock like the lawyer on TV?"

"Yeah weird I know, but that's his name."

"Well hell, that's a good sign."

"Maybe, but I'm going to give him a call. If anybody can get your friend out, it's Matlock."

"Please give me a call."

"Trey, let me warn you he is super expensive."

"Money is not an object. I need him out before —"

Dr. Rozelle cut him off. "Trey, careful what you say on these phones."

"Yeah you're right."

"Will call you back shortly."

Trey plopped down on the sofa. Trying to figure out what he was going to do next. He'd lost three hundred grand and he guessed he was going to have to spend more money to get Monte out, then an attorney. But money wasn't what he was thinking about, he had plenty of that. So much that he couldn't count it all. He'd attempted to count his stash once and he got tired after he reached two and a half million dollars and there was still a lot more to count. But he needed to get that situation with Monte under control so they could get back to work. There was a lot of money to be made in Atlanta. And he intended to get his share.

Starr entered the room, wearing a very fitted dress that looked as if it was shellacked to her ass and a pair of heels exposing her hot pink toe-nail polish. He loved when she wore pink, or any woman for that matter. It was so damn girly and Trey was very much a man. Treys eyes glued to Starr's ass. When she saw him staring, she smiled.

But his face was expressionless though he was clearly turned on. Why didn't he at least grab her ass?

"Trey, what's wrong babe?'

"Nothing."

"Come on, you know me."

"Hey listen, you don't need to be in my business. I've always told you, the less you know the better off we are."

She eased over and stood in front on him before unzipping his pants and taking him deep in her mouth.

Trey was trying to focus on Starr's spectacular oral abilities. She licked his shaft and sucked his balls but when she licked the head of his penis like she was licking an ice cream cone, he pushed her head down. She moved his hands. She hated when he did that. He stared at the ceiling, while Starr was still performing. The bell rang.

Starr stopped and they both looked at each other.

He said, "You expecting company?"

"No."

He stood and zipped his pants. He glanced through the peephole.

He said, "It's your friend's boyfriend."

"Who?"

"You know the girl with the fake ass."

"First of all, she is not my friend."

"Wonder what the hell he wants."

Starr said, "Open the door and find out."

Trey opened the door "What's up, bruh? What bring you here?" They bumped fists and Trey invited him in.

Shamari said, "Hey, Starr, how you doing?"

"I'm good? How you doing?"

Shamari said, "I need to talk to you for a second in private if you don't mind?"

Trey said, "For sho." He turned to Starr. "Give us a few moments alone."

Starr waved bye to Shamari and left the room. When she was gone, Shamari said, "Look, bruh, I need a real big favor if you can. If you can't

I'll understand."

"What is it?"

"I need a front."

Trey and Shamari had talked about doing some business in the past but it never came to fruition. Shamari had wanted Trey to come down on his prices, but Trey wasn't having it.

Trey said, "What kind of a front?"

"Man, whatever you can give me. I was supposed to get something from my Mexican connect but he never came through for me. Dude, I'm down to my last ten stacks. Whatever you can give me."

Trey said, "Man I just got took last night. I don't know if I can help you now."

Shamari said, "I understand."

Trey said, "Last time I spoke to you, you wanted to buy twelve keys. What happened?"

"Feds snatched up some of my folks, and I had a couple of losses."

Trey said, "Feds."

Shamari grinned, then said, "Im'ma keep it one hundred with you. One of my soldiers turned informant."

"So he snitching on you? I don't need no parts of the Feds," Trey said thinking about Monte. Knowing he had to hurry and get Monte out of that Houston jail before he cooperated with the Feds.

"Nobody is snitching on me."

"You sure?"

"I'm positive. He ain't snitching on nobody right now. If you get my drift?"

Trey smiled and said, "It has to be that way sometimes. Sometimes is best that they are gone, rather than to live to tell about it."

Shamari said, "Exactly."

Trey said, "Listen, bruh, I can't help you right now, but we are going to work for sure. As soon as I handle this situation, I'm going to help you out. I know it must've taken a lot for you to ask me for help."

"Had to swallow my pride, that's for damn sure."

Trey said, "Hold up, I got something for you." He sprinted upstairs and came back down with a purple crown royal bag and tossed it to Shamari.

"What's this?"

"Twelve thousand dollars. This should help you until we get going."

Shamari grinned and pounded Trey up and headed toward the door. Before he opened the door, he stopped. "Thanks again."

Trey nodded then Shamari opened the door and left. Trey eased over to the door and peeked through the blinds as he watched Shamari pull out of the driveway in the Range Rover, thinking Shamari was just like most dude's in Atlanta with their net worth tied up in their cars. Dude only had ten thousand dollars but drove a hundred thousand dollar car. Trey had always been good with money. He would never end up like Shamari.

CHAPTER 31

SHAMARI SMACKED JADA HARD ON HER ASS WHEN HE ENTERED THE house. She turned and faced him, frowning when he leaned into her and kissed her. Hands gripping her ass. She felt so good in his arms. He hadn't touched her in so long, she had forgotten how much she liked him to fuck her. When he stopped kissing her, she said, "Somebody is real happy."

Shamari's dick jumped and he looked down. "You talking about him."

Jada said, "He's always happy, I'm talking about you."

"Well I'm happy because money is on the way."

Jada said, "The Mexicans came through for you."

"No. Those motherfuckers lied."

"Damn."

"Yeah but it's okay, I don't really trip about money. I haven't always had money, so it's really not a big deal for me. I'm the same person with it or without it."

He hugged her and held her for a long time and she felt safe in his arms. She felt a certain closeness that she hadn't felt with him in a long time. When he released her he asked, "Have you seen your mom lately?"

Jada said, "No. Why?"

"Because I don't hear you talking about her. You never mention her anymore."

"I haven't seen her in a while and don't really want to see her. You know it's the same thing every time I see her. Her hand's always out. You know, always drinking and going off."

Shamari said, "Look, it don't matter if your mom drinks or not. She is still your mom. I wish I still had my mother, I damn sure wouldn't deny her."

Jada said, "I guess you're right. I'll go check her out tomorrow."

Shamari dug into his pocket and handed Jada two one hundred dollar bills. "Buy her some groceries or something."

Jada sighed, "I guess I really have to go see her now."

"You weren't going to go?"

"Not really."

"Shame on you, Jada Simone."

They both laughed. Jada's mom and sisters always called her Jada Simone. Shamari thought the fact that they called her by her full name was funny and country.

CHAPTER 32

JADA'S STEPFATHER CHARLES WAS A TALL WIRY MAN WITH A THICK grey goatee. He wore a dirt colored shirt and jeans that were too big for him. He stood there smiling, revealing several missing teeth. He invited her inside the tiny apartment on the West End of Atlanta. An old sofa and an armchair filled the tiny room along with an old school floor model television. Jada swatted a roach that had dove onto her shoulder when she entered the house. "Who the hell is that Charles?" Louise yelled from the back room.

"Jada Simone."

"What the hell does she want?" Louise asked.

Jada began to have second thoughts about coming over. Why had she listened to Shamari. She should have just stayed at home and blocked out any memory of a family. She hated this hand she was dealt. Seconds later Louise entered the room with a forty ounce Colt .45. "What the fuck do you want, bitch?"

"I love you too, Mom."

Charles said, "Louise, don't be mean. You haven't seen Jada in ages."

Louise took a swig of beer and said, "Fuck you and fuck this bitch." She then stared at Charles. "And if you want to defend this bitch, you can take yo ass to the Atlanta men's shelter. I pay the cost to be the boss in this motherfucker, and don't you forget it."

Charles sat his skinny ass on the sofa without uttering so much as another word to Louise. He knew when she was drunk not to say much because she would often become violent, and the first thing she would do would be to crack him upside his head with the forty-ounce bottle.

Louise turned her attention to Jada. "What the hell brings you here, Jada Simone?"

"Well, if you must know, I came to see how you're doing. Shamari told me to check on you."

"How is he doing?'

"Good."

Charles reached for Louise's forty ounce and she refused. "Get your own, motherfucker. There ain't no telling where your mouth has been."

Jada sat on the armchair.

"So you plan on staying?"

"Mom, why are you acting like this?"

"Like what?"

"I mean I'm coming over here to check on you and you act like you can care less about me."

"That's because I don't give a damn about yo ass."

Jada stood up from the chair; there was no way she was going to sit there and take too much more of Louise's abuse.

Louise said, "That's what the fuck I thought."

Jada said, "Why must every second word be a curse word?"

She stared at Jada then said, "Like I told Charles, I pay the cost to be the boss."

"I heard that every day when I was a little girl."

Louise said, "I raised you. I may not have been the best mama in the world, but I raised you and Lisa the best way I could and you ask me why I don't give a fuck about you?" She smacked Charles on his shoulder and said, "Scoot yo ass over." Charles moved to the very edge of the tiny sofa because Louise was a wide woman. Short in stature with a humongous ass and a cute brown face and a slight mustache that needed to be waxed.

Jada said, "Mom you gonna keep living in the past. There is no way we can repair what happened in the past."

"You the one keep holding my past against me—"

Charles had the nerve to turn the volume up on the TV and when Louise was drowned out, she slapped him in the mouth so hard that his lip started bleeding.

"Turn that goddamned TV down! Can't you see me and my daughter is talking. As a matter of fact, get the hell out of here!"

Charles stood, pants falling off his rail thin body. He said to Jada, "Good seeing you again."

"Likewise."

When he was gone, Louise said, "You think you're better than me and Lisa. You always have."

"That's not true, Mom."

"Well why don't you come see us? I tell you why, because you think you're better than us." Louise finished off the beer then burped loudly. "Well, I got news for you, Ms. White Woman, you ain't no better than us. You can live in that big house and drive all those expensive cars, but at the end of the day you still a nigger."

Jada sat back on the armchair. "I never thought I was better than nobody. But how you think I felt having a big sister on crack and a Mama that's an alcoholic."

"Lisa just got out of rehab and she has a job. You would know these things if you were part of the family."

"Well that's good."

"And the court gave her custody of Niya."

Niya was Jada's niece. Niya had been in and out of group homes because of Lisa's struggles with her drug addiction.

"How old is Niya now?"

Louise said, "That's a goddamned shame you don't know how old your own niece is."

"Well I haven't seen her in like three years."

"She's twelve, I think," Louise said then she yelled, "Charles come here."

Charles appeared with a wet spot on the front of his jeans.

Louise said, "Did you piss in yo clothes, nigga?"

Charles looked down and when he saw the wet spot he said, "I'll be damned."

"How old is Niya?"

"Eight."

"Hell no, Niya ain't eight! She got to be at least eleven or twelve. Lisa had her when she was twenty and she's 31 now."

"Oh yeah," Charles said staring down at the piss spot. Feeling embarrassed only because Jada was there.

Louise said, "Make yourself useful and grab me another beer."

Charles took off toward the kitchen and Louise said, "Not before you wash yo damn hands. Didn't you say you just pissed?"

Jada laughed. Her mama was a trip. Same old Louise paying the cost to be the boss. At that moment she realized how much she'd missed her mom.

When Louise saw Jada laughing, she smiled. "If this nigga had a brain, he'd be dangerous."

"Mama, you're crazy."

"And you're crazy too."

"The apple don't fall too far from the tree."

Louise smiled and said, "Come here and give me a damn hug."

Jada made her way over to the sofa and gave her Mama a big hug.

Louise said, "I know I wasn't the best mama in the world. But I tried my ass off. When yo no good ass daddy left me, I did what I had to do to put food on the table even if that meant selling ass. I made sure y'all had the best of everything."

Jada didn't want to hear about her mama selling ass but she knew that it was true. She remembered the men coming in and out of the house every day when she was growing up. But she and Lisa always had the best of everything growing up. The best clothes. They kept their hair done. Always the latest Jordan's when she was in the Tom-Boy phase of her life.

"Mama, I don't want to hear about you selling ass."

Louise smiled. "You know what I don't want to hear about?"

"What?"

"I don't want to hear about how life was fucked up for you growing up? That's the past. Can we work on the future?"

Jada said, "I guess we can."

Louise and Jada hugged each other, neither wanting to let each other go.

Charles appeared with the beer. Standing there looking dumb. Finally he twisted the top off the beer. Louise let go of Jada and said, "Motherfucker, I wish you would put your lips on my goddamned beer."

CHAPTER 33

LANI SAT AT THE TABLE EATING BAKED CHICKEN AND BROWN RICE when Chris came in and said, "Your motherfuckin' ex had something to do with me getting robbed."

"Huh?"

"Yeah, Black had this shit set up."

Lani scooped some rice with her fork and said, "What the hell are you talking about. Black don't know shit about your business." She drank some water then said, "Wait a goddamned minute! Are you saying I had something to do with what happened?"

Chris took a seat at the table and said, "Hell no, babe. Never would I ever think you would do anything like that. I'm just saying—"

"Saying what?"

"Me and Mike found Rodriguez and fucked him up pretty badly. He told us that Kyrie and Black put him up to doing this."

Lani dropped her fork. "Are you serious?"

"I'm dead serious?"

"So Rodriguez knows Black."

"Well he and Kyrie are cousins."

"I don't believe that."

Chris said, "Why I gotta lie about this?"

Lani said, "This just doesn't sound like Black, that's all. I was with him for a long time and I've never known him to rob anybody. I mean this dude got money. Why would he have to rob anybody?"

"Come on Lani, I know that's your boy but he don't like me and you know it." Chris stood from the table and said, "I can't believe you even defending this dude."

Lani said, "I'm going to get to the bottom of this."

Chris said, "You stay out of this!"

"What are you gonna do?"

"I don't know what I'm gonna do, but I don't need you asking him about shit. That will put him on alert."

"What about Rodriguez, you don't think he's gonna say anything?"

"What is he gonna say? 'I told Chris that you put me up to doing this bullshit.' That will get him killed. Naw, he ain't gonna say shit."

Lani pushed her plate aside. She couldn't finish her food. She didn't want to believe the man that she had once loved had done something so damn cruel. Now her current love was out for revenge. There was no doubt in her mind that Chris and Mike were going to get revenge. But how? She just hoped nobody would get hurt too bad.

CHAPTER 34

IT WAS 2:30 WHEN TREY STROLLED IN TO DR. ROZELLE'S OFFICE carrying a briefcase with a hundred thousand dollars.

Dr. Rozelle was a small white man with thinning hair and expensive eyeglasses. He had a permanent look of skepticism on his face and he was always thoughtful before he spoke. He stood and closed the blinds, then he shook Trey's hand.

"Good to see you?"

"Same here?'

"Did you bring the cash?"

"Yeah, I didn't know what to bring, so I brought a hundred thousand dollars."

"Well, you're going to need another twenty thousand."

"Why so much?"

"Matlock's fees are ridiculous, plus your friend is not from Texas, so most bondsman won't touch him, but Matlock has one that will."

"Okay I'll have to bring it back to you later."

"Bring me big bills this time?"

Trey said, "Yeah, it's mostly hundreds. There are a few fives and tens."

Dr. Rozelle sighed and said, "Jesus Christ, Trey, you make my job so hard."

"I'm sorry, man. I mean that's all I had."

"I have been telling you for years. Start a business, a cash business. A dry cleaners, pay taxes on the money, and write checks."

"Yeah but I don't want to be associated with this case. You know that."

"You would write the check to me, and I would write one to Matlock."

"Listen, I'm gonna take your advice. The next time I need you, I will write a check"

Dr. Rozelle thought for a moment then he said, "When Monte gets out, don't say a word to him."

"He doesn't know where you live right?"

"Never been to my house."

"Good"

•   •   •

Jada was dressed in a simple white blouse and skinny jeans with a leather jacket and the wedges that Craig had purchased for her. Craig greeted her with a big hug when she entered Halo, a local lounge with a chic ambience. He led her to a table in the back corner of the lounge. She ordered an apple martini and he ordered water.

"Not drinking today?"

He said, "Trying to lose ten pounds."

She said, "Not fair that I'm drinking and you're not. You trying to make me look like a slush."

"Not at all, just trying to stay in shape. I'm approaching my 50th birthday and I damn sure don't want to look 50."

The server came back with the drinks and Jada said, "I don't think it's a good idea for us to keep seeing each other?"

"Why not?"

She sipped her martini and said, "I just feel so guilty."

"You shouldn't feel guilty."

"But I love Shamari. You just don't understand. I love this man. I owe this man; he was there for me when I didn't have nobody. He pulled me out of a bad situation."

Craig sipped his water. He knew that no matter how much money he spent on her, it would hardly create the kind of bond she had with her man. Hell they were from the same place. They were the same color.

"You don't understand do you?"

"Actually I do. My wife Anne was there for me when I didn't have a damn thing. Even though things have been really vanilla lately with our sex life, I feel indebted to her."

"Indebted is not the same as guilty."

"True." Craig was quiet. Taking it all in, he didn't want to stop seeing her. He flagged the waitress and said, "Give me a scotch on the rocks." He took a deep breath and then said, "I really need a drink now."

The waitress came back and sat the drink in front of him.

She said, "I had sex with him the other day, and I realized how much I missed him holding me."

Craig sipped his drink then said, "I can give you a better life and you know this."

Jada said, "Did you know my mama was an alcoholic?"

"No."

"So is my stepdad."

"Really?"

"My sister is an ex-crack head."

"Okay where are you going with this?"

"This is a lifestyle you wouldn't understand."

"No. Can't say that I would, but what does that have to do with me and you?"

"It has everything to do with me and you. We're not the same; I can tell Shamari about this because his family is just as fucked up as mine. He understands me."

"You're saying y'all are more compatible?"

"Yes."

"Can we be friends? Platonic?"

"I don't think that's a good idea."

"Why not?"

"Because I am attracted to you. But not in that way."

"So you're going to cut me out of your life."

"Don't look at it like that. You're still my favorite surgeon." She stood and said, "I have to go."

He stared at her, observing how her jeans were gripping her ass. His mind went back to the sex on top of the Maserati. He didn't say anything as she walked away, but there was no way he would let this beautiful ass woman walk out of his life.

Black was pulling out of a neighborhood in southeast Atlanta when a Chevy Volt pulled alongside his Porsche. When he noticed the men wearing ski mask, he knew it was bad news. They opened fire. Sixteen shots fired into the side of Black's Porsche. He lost control on the steering wheel and hit a telephone pole. The men sped off. A concerned citizen driving a Jeep Cherokee tried to call 911 before a shot was fired into his car barely missing his head. The operator was on the line. The concerned citizen gave 911 the whereabouts of the incident. The paramedics were there a few minutes later, along with the firemen. The Porsche was so mangled, they had to cut the car open to remove Black from the car. Black was barely breathing. They transported him to Grady Memorial.

It was 2:00 when Lani got a call from Nana, Black's grandmother.

"Hello."

"Hey I was just calling to tell you that Tyrann is in the hospital and it ain't looking too good."

"What happened?"

"He got shot this morning. That's all I know. I told that chile to get out of the drug business."

Lani didn't say anything. She knew what had happened, Mike and Chris had retaliated. Though Black brought this on his self, she felt bad about the whole situation.

Nana said, "I know you and Tyrann ain't seeing each other no mo, but I thought you might want to know about this. I'm sorry if I bothered you."

"No Nana. I have been meaning to come see you anyway. Other than this terrible news, how have you been?"

"Well I lost one of my breasts but I been hanging in there. The best a woman my age can do."

"Tyrann didn't tell me that."

"You kidding me? I always tell him to tell you I'm thinking about you and think you're the best girlfriend he ever had."

"Thank you Nana."

"I'm going back up to the hospital to see Tyrann. He's in the intensive care unit if you want to come see him. Grady Memorial Hospital."

"Okay Nana." Lani didn't want to commit to going to see Black.

"And if you ain't able to come see him, I'll understand, but please pray for him."

Lani said, "I will." She ended the call.

CHAPTER 35

WHEN CHRIS ENTERED THE HOUSE LANI SAID, "WHAT THE FUCK HAVE you done?"

Chris said, "What are you talking about?"

"Black got shot this morning. I suppose you didn't have shit to do with it."

"Maybe. Maybe not."

"What the fuck do you mean maybe? Maybe not?"

Chris made eye contact with Lani. "Let me get this straight. This nigga damned near killed me, and you worried about that bitch ass nigga."

"He didn't shoot you."

"He threatened me at your mama's house."

Chris licked his chapped lips. Not wanting to respond to Lani. Couldn't believe this chick was going on about this nigga.

"Why did you shoot him?"

"I ain't shoot nobody."

"You had him shot?"

"You don't know that."

"Dude, I hope you know if he dies, you got a murder case on your head."

Chris said, "You must still be fucking this dude. Why the fuck are you worried about him? I don't remember you being this worried about me when I was in the hospital."

"You were in a coma. You don't remember shit."

Chris paced the floor, wanting to slap the shit out of Lani. But he'd never hit a woman and he never would. He didn't get down like that.

Lani approached Chris and wrapped her arms around him and said, "Did you have to take it to that level?"

Chris removed her arms and said, "He tried to kill me."

Lani said, "You put me in a bad position. I know his family and they're calling me, asking me to come see him at the hospital."

Chris leaned against the door and said, "Is that so?"

"Well, his Nana called me."

"I told you a long time ago if he kept fucking with me, his Nana was going to be burying him."

Lani thought about the possibility of Nana having to bury Black. She didn't want to think about that, but she knew that if Black was able to walk out of that hospital, he was going to retaliate. This stupid ass war would go on forever.

Lani said, "Was all of this worth it?"

Chris said, "I lost money and time when they put me in the hospital."

Lani said, "I'm sorry about that."

Chris said, "Are you really sorry? A few minutes ago you were worried about his old gray ass Nana."

Lani slapped the shit out of Chris. She'd slapped him so hard you could see her hand print on the side of his face.

When she realized what she'd done she came to his side and said, "I'm sorry."

Chris said, "Get the fuck away from me, Lani."

Lani wouldn't budge so Chris shoved her to the floor.

"So you're beating women now."

"I didn't do shit to you, you're the one that hit me."

Lani picked herself up off the floor, stood in his personal space again and he pushed her again and she yelled.

"If you put another goddamned hand on me, I'm gonna call the police on yo ass."

"Huh?" Chris laughed and said, "You're fuckin' tripping man."

"Motherfucker, try me and see who's tripping."

Chris said, "I'm getting the fuck out of here."

Lani said, "Me too. I'll be at the hospital seeing Black."

Chris said, "Tell his folks I will be praying for his black ass."

Trey and Starr was turning in the parking lot of Lenox Mall when they noticed a Toyota Prius flashing its lights, trying to get their attention. When Trey gave his car to the valet, the Prius was right behind him. Monte jumped out of the Prius. Trey said, "What the hell are you doing out?"

"I got out two days ago, dawg. Man, that lawyer you got me was the truth. They are going to put me on house arrest here until I go to court."

Trey had just given Dr. Rozelle the money three days ago. Damn he must've gotten out the next day. Dr. Rozelle must have been unaware of this or he would have called Trey and told him.

Monte handed the valet the keys to the Prius then turned to Trey and said, "You're going to pay for this right. I ain't got shit."

"Yeah I got ya."

A young black guy reluctantly took the keys to the Prius. Looking like he knew he damn sure wasn't going to get a tip for this car.

Starr stood there looking cute, wondering if Trey was going to make an introduction. And was wondering what all this lawyer talk was about. Something must have gone bad.

Monte introduced himself to Starr.

"I'm Starr."

Monte smiled and said, "You damn sure are." His eyes on Starr's thighs. The black tights she wore made her look amazing and those riding boots elevated that ass.

Monte kept grinning until it made Starr uncomfortable, not because he was ugly but because he'd basically raped her with his eyes.

"So you're the Kingpin's wife."

Trey said, "Would you shut the fuck up, and quit disrespecting my girl."

Monte said, "Can't a nigga dream?"

Trey handed Starr fifty one-hundred dollar bills and said, "Go ahead without me, babe. I need to talk to Monte."

Starr headed to Neiman Marcus. When she was out of sight, Trey said, "What the hell happened?"

Monte presented him with the police report.

Trey and Monte sat on a bench in the middle of the mall as Trey read over the report:

Officer Brad Williams was cruising on Interstate 45 when he noticed a red Toyota Camry swerving and following too close when he pulled the suspects over. Suspect Rogers appeared to be nervous, and suspect Parker failed to make eye contact with him. Officer Williams noted that he thought that was odd. Officer Williams then removed Rogers and Parker from the car, noticing that Parker's pants were unzipped and Parker's hair was disheveled. He believed but didn't have any proof that they'd been engaging in some kind of sexual activity. Williams separated Rogers and Parker. He asked each of them how long they'd been in Texas and what they were there for, and their stories were wildly inconsistent. Parker stated they'd been there for four days, and Rogers said they'd been there for two days. In addition Rogers said he was visiting a friend and Parker said, she was there to visit her sister who attended the University of Houston. Officer Williams then summoned the K9 unit and was alarmed when the dog indicated that something was in the door panel. 10 kilos of coke were found in the door panels.

Trey said, "Who the hell is Shantelle Parker?"

Monte said, "Look man I know you're going to be mad at me, but all I can say is I fucked up."

Trey said, "What the fuck did you take somebody with you for?"

"Look I know you told me to go alone."

"What the fuck were you thinking?"

"Look, I swear to you this is the only time I've done this. I've always gone by myself."

"Where is the girl?"

"She's out. I told them that she didn't know shit about this and told them to let her out."

"They let her go?"

"Yeah, I think she was released the same day."

"Well that's good."

Monte made eye contact with Trey. "You know me man, this is all on me, dawg. Nobody is going down but me."

Trey stared at the paperwork. Rogers's pants were unzipped and Parker's hair was disheveled. "What the fuck, were you getting head?"

"No." Monte giggled and looked at Trey who didn't think it was funny. Monte then said, "Come on, man, you know I ain't that motherfuckin' stupid."

"Dude, I didn't think you were dumb enough to take somebody down to Texas with you."

"Look, man, I wasn't getting head."

"Why was this bitch's hair disheveled?"

"Hey, it was just a country ass hairstyle."

"Whatever, dude." Trey stared Monte in the face and said, "If I find out that you were getting head and got pulled over, it's gonna be bad on you."

"Trey." Monte looked frightened. Wondering what the hell Trey meant by gonna be bad on him.

"What do you want?"

"I wasn't getting head. That's stupid."

Trey said, "So what do you want now?"

"I need money man. I ain't got shit. I need to pay my bills."

"Ok, so is that why you felt the need to chase me down," Trey said, still staring at the paper, wondering if this idiot got pulled over because he was getting head. This would be a goddamned shame if he lost over two hundred thousand dollars because of something like this."

Starr came running back to the spot where Trey and Monte were. She could tell they were still in deep conversation and she didn't want to interrupt. She said, "Baby, I'll be in Bebe's."

Trey said, "I thought you hate that store."

"I do, but my friend Sharee works there. I wanna holla at her."

Starr walked to Bebe's, Monte's eyes following her ass in those tight ass skinny jeans and 5 inch heels.

When Trey saw him staring, he slapped the fuck out him.

Monte grabbed his mouth and said, "Trey, what the hell you do that for?"

"First of all, you looking at my woman's ass and secondly, all you think about is ass. You probably were getting head or something when the cops pulled yo dumb ass over."

Monte said, "Trey, bruh, believe me that ain't the case."

Trey said, "So what do you want? I got you out and paid for your attorney."

"I know, but I don't have any cash. I ain't got shit."

"Motherfucker, you've made almost 200,000 dollars in the last six months. Where the hell did that money go?"

Monte shrugged, "You know, the more money you make the more you fuck up."

Trey said, "Give me your new number and I'll call you when I leave the mall. I'm enjoying the rest of the evening with my lady."

Monte said, "The cops kept my phone. I ain't got no phone."

Trey removed a wad of cash from his pocket, peeled off 10 one hundred dollar bills and passed them to Monte.

Monte said, "Thanks, but how do I get in touch with you?"

Trey stood up from the bench, picturing Monte getting head while driving with ten kilos of coke in the car. How could this motherfucker be so stupid?

Monte reached for the paperwork and Trey said, "I'm going to keep this."

"Ok, that's fine, but how am I gonna get in touch with you again?" Monte said.

Trey said, "There is no need to be in touch with me. You're out. You've been paid."

Monte said, "So you're not going to give me nothing else."

"Like what?"

"Money."

"Hell no, nigga! I've lost over three hundred stacks fucking with you."

Monte said, "Do you still live in the same place?"

"Huh?"

"You still live in the same house."

Trey's mind raced wondering if Monte knew where he resided. He suddenly remembered that he'd directed Monte to his home one night after a run from Houston. Damn, this was bad.

"Yeah why? I live in the same house. Why you ask?"

"Just in case I need some more money for legal fees."

"Didn't I tell you that the lawyer was paid in full?"

Starr came running back with two bags in her hand.

Trey said, "Monte, I'll holla at you later."

Monte headed toward the exit of the mall, before he reached the door, he turned and glanced at Starr's ass.

• • •

Lani walked to the edge of hospital room 333 to witness Nana praying over Black, who lay in the bed unconscious. She'd bowed her head and said, "God, I know Tyrann hasn't been the best of servants, but he's a good person with good intentions. Lord, I'm not asking you to save Tyrann's life if it's not your will. I want your will to be done. I just want to say that I've raised him since he was eight years old and now he's thirty three years old. I know you know this, you're God, I'm an OLD LADY now and I've had many blessings in my life and I lived to see my great-great grandkids and I couldn't be more thankful. I've fought and beaten breast cancer. I stand here before you with one breast, but thankful to you that I'm still here at eighty-three years old. Like I say, Lord, let your will be done, but if Tyrann passes, it will destroy me, for he is my favorite grandchild and he's all I live for. Father, let your will be done. When Nana was done with her prayer, Lani was in tears. She'd decided not to go into the room. She headed to her car but before cranking it up, she decided to go back up to the hospital room. Nana was asleep with an old tattered bible across her lap. Lani then walked over to Black's bed and kissed him on the forehead. She still loved that man. How could she not. He had helped her for so long financially and had done so much for her family. She didn't want him to die. She left the hospital before Nana would wake up.

• • •

Shamari and Jada were lying in the bed facing one another. She wore a purple G-string and bra set and he wore nothing but his boxers. She was tracing his back with her long nails. His hand planted firmly on the cusp of her ass. The vanilla spray she wore had him mesmerized. Though she had so many kinds of expensive perfumes, he loved when she wore vanilla. She said, "What ever happened with the situation with Tony?"

"I don't know what happened. The attorney hasn't said anything. I'm assuming he's keeping his mouth shut. I'm not worrying about that right now." He sucked her neck.

Her finger was in the hole in the front of his underwear. She felt his manhood swell. She wanted him. She hadn't had him in a long while, but she couldn't help but think about Tony. She said, "So you don't think about going to jail?"

"No. I think about being broke. Do I want to go to jail? No. But I don't want to be broke either."

She said, "I don't know what I would do if something happened to you."

He placed his hands over her lips and said, "You're killing the mood."

"I just love you so much, Shamari."

He said, "How things go with your Mom?"

She burst out laughing thinking about her visit.

"What's so funny?"

"Just thinking about what mama did to Charles."

Shamari laughed, trying to pull that small ass G-string down, but was having trouble cuz he was staring at her ass at the same time. It looked spectacular with the tiny string literally hidden between that big bubble.

She said, "I know, mama is so funny." She helped him with the G-string, then she removed the bra. The implants making her breasts stand at attention. Nipples very erect.

"I'm glad you went over there."

She smiled, "I'm glad you talked me into going."

Shamari said, "Look, no matter who our parents are, we gotta be thankful. Always be thankful. Don't ever forget where you came from."

She smiled because he knew her so damn well. She removed his boxer and licked the shaft of his erect penis.

Shamari ran his hand through her expensive weave. Jada hummed on his balls.

He said, "Please stop, it feels too damn good."

She laughed and he pulled her on top of him and inserted himself inside.

She rode him for a while before going reverse cowboy, which he loved, because he loved looking at her ass.

His hands on her backside as she went up and down.

He ordered her to get down. " I wanna please you."

She laid on her back, his head now between her thighs and she closed her legs and said, "Let me get cleaned up before you do all that."

He pried them open and said, "Come on, babe, we been in this too long for you to be getting all fancy on me."

She giggled then her legs collapsed. He licked her inner thigh and she pushed his head further down until his tongue was on her clit. She moaned and he kept licking her and she swayed her hips forward until she was fucking his face. She said, "Damn, baby, you're feeling so goddamn good to me."

"I love you, baby," he said.

"I love you too."

Shamari fingered her pussy good while his tongue still worked her clit. He then flipped her over on her stomach and ran his tongue in between her ass crack. She hollered and said, *"Craig you feel so goddamned good to me!*

Shamari said, "What did you say? What did you call me?"

• • •

It was 5 am when Trey heard the front door crashing in. "Intruder! Intruder!" the alarm said. Trey opened the nightstand drawer. Fishing around in the dark before he found his 9mm. "Who the fuck is that?" He felt stupid for even asking who it was. It was very unlikely that they would answer.

Starr was lying there butt naked looking at Trey in the dark before turning the lamp switch on. She stood looking for her bedroom shoes. Trey making sure there were bullets in the clip.

Starr said, "The police are on the way."

"Intruder! Intruder! Intruder!"

Someone yelled, "We are the goddamned police! Come out with your goddamned hands up!"

What the fuck were the police there for? Nobody called them.

Starr peeked through the blinds and said, "Baby, that is the police; there are about twenty fucking cars out there.

Trey's heart pounded fast as he thought about that stupid ass Monte asking if he still lived in the same place. But there were no drugs or money here. They could search all the fuck they wanted. They would come up with nothing.

That stupid ass alarm was sounding "Intruder" Intruder" Intruder!"

"This is Officer Martin! Come out with your hands up or we're shooting!"

Trey said, "There's no need for that. I'm coming out!" He placed the gun on the dresser and said, "I'm coming out."

He removed a t-shirt from the dresser drawer and after it was on, he opened the door.

The officer yelled. "I wanna see your goddamned hands!"

Trey waved his hands. A tall white officer with a handlebar mustache tackled Trey and handcuffed him.

A black female officer was ordered to handcuff Starr.

Trey said, "Can you tell me what this about?

A bald black plainclothes officer said, "Shut the fuck up. We ask the questions."

Trey made eye contact with Starr while he was lying on the floor. She was complaining about the cuffs being too tight. A single tear rolled down her face.

Trey said, "Fuck."

- PART FOUR -

PART FOUR

CHAPTER 36

SHAMARI STOOD UP FROM THE BED, HIS ERECTION SHRIVELED AND only semi-hard. Not because he wasn't attracted to her, because he very much wanted to dive inside her nicely shaved pussy, but she'd said something alarming, and he wanted clarification.

He said, "Babe, what did you say? Who is Craig?"

Oh fuck, Jada thought. "I don't know who Craig is. Why are you asking me this?"

"You said, 'Craig you feel so goddamned good to me.' "

She giggled and said, "I said this *head* feels so goddamned good to me."

Shamari laughed and said, "I thought you were calling me another nigga's name." With his dick now limp, he eased into the bathroom and peed before cleaning his penis with a towel. He washed his hands and returned to the bedroom. He saw Jada sitting on the edge of the bed with her chin in the palms of her hands.

"What's wrong?"

"You stopped the foreplay."

"I thought you called me by somebody else's name, and it killed the mood."

"Why would I do that?"

He sat next to her. "Besides, I've got a lot on my mind."

She looked at him. "Please tell me."

He sighed. He didn't feel like going into the details of his life, especially details about his drug business.

"You never tell me shit nowadays," she said.

He turned away from her and then stood. He grabbed his briefs lying on the floor and slipped them on.

"What the fuck is going on, Shamari?"

"Im'ma tell you." He made eye contact with her. "Just give me a chance."

"Tell me now, goddamn it."

"Well—"

She cut him off. "Are you going to jail? Did that Tony motherfucker tell on you?" She stood and paced. "I knew you shouldn't have done that bullshit. You're not in the goddamn Mafia. You've let this life go to your goddamn head."

Shamari took hold of her arm her and said, "Will you shut the fuck up please?"

"I'm sorry, baby. You know I like to know what's going on."

"It has nothing to do with Tony," he paused then said, "well not directly."

"Why are you dragging this shit out?"

"Finances, babe."

"What about them?"

"Financial problems. The money ain't flowing and there was too much going out, and now, we don't have shit coming in."

"What do you mean?"

"I'm broke." He paused and looked away. She could tell this was really hard for him to talk about, but she needed him to be forthcoming. She didn't want to nag, but she didn't want him to shut down.

He faced her again. "Yeah, the money is gone."

"I know you mentioned all the money you'd spent on Tony's attorney about a week ago, but you said you still had about fifty grand."

"Well I lied." There was an awkward silence. "I don't have fifty cents," he said.

She stared at him but didn't say anything.

Shamari continued, "I'm really broke. I mean, I borrowed some money, but I have to pay it back. I have nothing personally."

"What happened?"

"I told you what happened!" he shouted. She looked sad, almost as if she were about to cry so he said, "I'm sorry."

She said, "That's okay." Then she said, "If there's anything I can do to help, let me know. I can sell all my shoes and bags. I know I can come up with some money to help you. I've got at least a hundred thousand dollars worth of shoes and shit I don't wear. Hell, some of that shit, I've never worn. And I already told you I would sell the watch."

"You would do that for me?"

"I would do anything for you." Though Jada had been fucking another man behind Shamari's back, she wouldn't hesitate to help him. He'd done so much for her over the years that there was no way she wouldn't help him if she could.

"I think we're going to be okay."

"You think?"

He laughed, "Would you leave me if I went broke?"

She said, "According to you, you're already broke. Have I gone anywhere?"

She sat back on the bed, her nipples hard. She covered herself with the sheets.

He lay on the bed beside her.

"You know I hate when you lay on top of the covers and I'm underneath."

He slid underneath the covers with her. She ran her fingers through his hair and said, "What is going on?"

"The Mexicans cut me off. I have no connect."

"So basically, if I did sell all of my things, you still wouldn't have a supplier."

"Things are going to be okay." He said that confidently and she wanted to believe him but she didn't. He'd been down and out before, and she'd seen him go from nothing to millions of dollars several times, but she wasn't sure this time. His swag was different. He seemed defeated.

"I can't help but worry. With all that is going on with Tony attempting to murder that informant. Then, the Feds came to pick you up for questioning and now you're telling me that we ain't got shit..."

Shamari said, "I didn't want to tell you this, but I spoke to Trey and he's going to help us out."

"Who?"

"Your girlfriend Starr's man, Trey."

"She's Lani's friend."

"Well I'm going to work with Trey until I can get back on my feet."

"Oh, well now Starr is going to be all up in our fucking business."

"What are you talking about?"

"I'm saying she's going to know our financial situation."

"This is hustling. Everybody has ups and downs."

Jada sprang from the bed. "This is some nigga shit. I mean on the surface, we're doing good. You drive a Bentley and now you're telling me we're broke." She giggled and then said, "How crazy is that?"

"Yeah! A Bentley that's about to get repossessed. I'm trying to sell it before that happens."

She huffed and said, "I can't believe this shit."

"A minute ago you were telling me that you were going to sell whatever you had to help me get back in position. Now you're mad." He stood and shrugged, "I don't get it."

"I don't want Starr all in my business." She walked to the other side of the room and opened the dresser removing a pair of pink shorts with the words *Love Pink* written across the ass. She slid into them, along with one of his t-shirts that swallowed her and covered her butt.

"I didn't want to tell you this at first, but I had to. I didn't want to keep anything away from you"

"I'm glad you told me the truth. But we're going to have to do better. Man, this is unbelievable! We're living in this big-ass house, driving all these fancy-ass cars, and we don't have nothing!"

Shamari said, "It happens sometimes. It's called hustling."

"You mean hustling backwards!"

"Yeah you're right." Shamari felt like a complete fool for blowing through all of his money.

"We're getting older. I don't wanna keep doing this."

"What are you saying?"

"I can't do this any longer."

"But you knew what you were getting into when you met me. You knew I was a hustler."

"Yeah, but have you ever thought about doing something else?"

"What the fuck am I gonna do, Jada? What can I do? I'm a black man with a criminal past. You want me to work at KFC at 31 years old. Get the fuck out of here."

"KFC niggas got more money than you!"

"That's a goddamned low blow, Jada!"

She sat beside him on the bed and brushed his hair with her hand and said. "I'm sorry, I'm with you for the long haul, but you got to leave this shit alone. You have to get out of this business."

He stared at her. "It's all I know. I've been doing this since I was twelve."

"Well, it's time to retire."

"And do what?"

"You can go back to school."

"And you're going to wait on me to go back to school?"

"I'll go with you." It sounded good and she probably could benefit from going back, but she knew she wasn't going to go back and neither was he.

He placed his hands around her tiny-ass waist and pulled her close to him and kissed her.

Then he stopped and said, "Jada, I wanna ask you something."

She kissed him again and said, "Anything."

"Who the fuck is Craig?"

"What?"

"I swear you said Craig."

"I said *head.*"

He unleashed his dick from his boxers and said, "Well, since you brought it up."

She laughed before taking him deep into her mouth.

CHAPTER 37

JADA WAS SURPRISED TO SEE LANI ON HER DOORSTEP. SHE HUGGED her and gave an air kiss before inviting her in. "What's going on? Haven't heard from you in a while."

"Where do I begin?"

"Begin wherever you wanna. I got time."

"Black, my ex, got shot a couple of nights ago, and he's not doing too well."

Jada said, "Damn, I always liked Black. I thought you were too good for him, but he was a good dude. I hope he's going to be okay."

"It's looking pretty damn bad right now, but if it's anybody who can pull though, it's him."

"My prayers are with him. What else is new?"

"Starr and Trey went to jail yesterday, and they're still in jail."

"What? Why?"

"Yeah, I don't know exactly what happened. I got a call from Starr's sister, Meeka, asking me what happened? The police raided their house this morning. I don't know if they got drugs or money or what. Nobody knows anything right now."

Jada wondered if Shamari knew this. She would have to tell him. The last thing he needed was to get caught up in some more shit. She would tell him when he came back home.

Lani was silent for a moment, and then she said. "I hope everything is okay with Starr."

Jada didn't respond. She could care less what happened to Starr, but she knew that Trey was going to help Shamari out, so she hoped it was nothing serious.

Jada led Lani into the kitchen, where they sat at the bar. Jada passed Lani a glass of lemonade and then asked. "So, what do you know about Black getting shot?"

"What makes you think I know something?"

"Well, Chris got robbed a few weeks ago, and now this."

Lani said, "You and Starr know me so goddamn well." She sipped her lemonade then said, "Chris had Black shot."

"What the fuck?"

"Black started the bullshit." Lani took a swig and said, "He had Chris robbed."

"Why?"

Lani shrugged. "Who the fuck knows? This shit is childish to me. You know how niggas can be. I think Black knows Chris has just as much money as he does, and his ego got in the way. He wants to take what Chris has."

Jada said, "You know damn well all this is about you. Why don't you just admit it?"

"Maybe it started out about me, but not anymore. They both are so goddamn childish."

Jada said, "Ain't nothing childish about gunshots fired and somebody almost getting murdered"

"Black still loves me."

"I know. What the fuck did you do to that man?"

There was a long pause as Lani thought about Black and the possibility of him dying. There was no way she would be able to forget this if he died. He had to pull through.

"Girl, what are you thinking about?"

"Huh?"

"You just zoned out."

"Well I was just hoping and wishing Black don't die."

"Try praying!"

"Well, that's another thing. I overheard Nana praying that he pull through. Black can do no wrong in that woman's eyes."

"I wish I still had my nana."

"His nana is more like his mother than his nana. She raised him. And he's taken really good care of her ever since he started hustling. He bought her a nice little house in South West Atlanta."

"Now tell me. What happened to Starr?"

"I don't know what is up with them."

Jada sighed and said, "That chick can't stand me."

"Why you say that?"

"She so goddamned judgmental. And I really don't like being around her, but I know she's your friend. Just know that I don't like her, and I know she don't like me."

Lani said, "Everybody is a little self righteous."

"I ain't feeling her."

"That's your right. You don't have to be around her."

"Shamari and Trey is doing business now."

"That don't mean you gotta hang out with her."

"Exactly."

"I didn't know Trey and Shamari were close friends."

"They're not BFFs. I think they met at your birthday party. They'd tried to do some business before and it didn't work out."

Lani looked confused. "Okay, so why now? Why are they doing business now?"

Jada said, "We're broke. Flat broke."

"Seriously?"

"Yeah. A lot of shit has happened. A lot of shit I ain't been talking about."

"Well, I know Shamari had gotten picked up by the Feds for questioning."

"Yeah," Jada said. Then she looked away briefly. Trying to decide how much information about the situation she wanted to disclose.

"Now you're the one looking spaced out."

Jada turned and met Lani's gaze. Then she said, "Shamari's friend attempted to kill a snitch, and they wanted to know if Shamari had anything to do with it."

"Did he?"

"How would I know that?"

"Hell, because he's your man!"

Lani stood, walked to the refrigerator, and refilled her glass from the dispenser. When she sat back at the table, she made eye contact again. "You know we've been knowing each other since the second grade. You know you can tell me anything," said Lani.

"Look, I don't know." Jada would never let anybody know what she knew about the hit.

"Now I told you everything about what's going on with Black and Chris, and you can't tell me what's really going on with Shamari?"

"What the fuck do you wanna know so bad for? I don't get it."

"Whoa! You're taking your goddamned frustration out on the wrong person. All I'm saying is that I tell you everything. I mean everything, and you always so goddamned secretive."

"I'm sorry, but that's not something I want to discuss right now."

"I understand, but I'm your friend. I've known about your fine-assed doctor you've been fucking, and I haven't said shit about that, have I?"

"I guess you're right, but that fucking nosey-ass Starr knows and she is one person too many."

"Starr has her own problems. Trey has a baby."

"What're you talking about?"

"Let me tell you. Starr's sister, Meeka, accidentally told me this morning that Starr just learned Trey has a son."

"What the fuck?"

"Now that's just between me and you. I can't believe Starr didn't tell me."

"Who am I gonna tell? I don't know nobody that bitch knows."

"Well don't even tell Shamari."

"Trust me. I got more shit to worry about than to be worrying about what the hell they got going in their household."

"I hear ya."

She finished her lemonade and then said, "I'm tired of this goddamned life."

"We gotta get out before it gets too late."

"Craig wants me to be with him. He keeps showing me this amazing life he can give me."

"He wants you to be his mistress, you mean?"

"Well yeah, I don't even think I can be with a white man, especially in Atlanta, and especially since I've dated mostly D-boys. I'm bound to see them all over the place. And I hear them now saying 'Jada Simone is with a white man.' "

"Who gives a fuck what the haters say?"

There was a long pause. As bad as Jada wanted to say she didn't give a fuck what the haters said about her, she cared. She cared a little too much. She was thirty-one years old with no skills. What else could she be but a kept woman? She knew this situation with Shamari was about to be over.

"Is the money the only reason you thinking about leaving Shamari?"

"No, not at all. I told him that I would sell my jewels and handbags to help him out. I know I could come up with at least a hundred grand to give him." Jada said

"You would do that for him?"

"Hell, the fuck yeah! Shamari is my *dude!* I'd give my right tit for that man and I'll always have love for him. No matter what."

"So why are you thinking about bailing? I have a feeling it has something to do with the Feds picking him up the other day." Lani paused when she saw Jada getting annoyed. She gulped her drink quickly and then said, "Is Shamari going to jail?"

"Now how would I know?"

"You may have a feeling something is wrong. You been around this long enough that you know when something is not quite right."

"I don't know. I really don't know what's happening with him." Jada stood and said, "I think you should leave."

"Fine," Lani said and got up to leave. Jada escorted her to the door and gave her a hug before Lani left.

CHAPTER 38

CRAIG AND JADA MET AT TWIST, ONE OF THE CITY'S MOST POPULAR restaurants, for drinks during their lunch. Craig drank water because he had to go back to work while Jada had a lemon drop Martini. She had dressed down today, but she still looked amazing in black leggings and heels that made her legs look extra long. Her pink lip gloss made Craig think about head. She sipped her martini and said, "I wanna go somewhere tropical."

"Like a vacation?"

"Yes," she smiled, "why not?" Her youthful exuberance made him feel young at that moment.

"How are you gonna get away?"

"No, how are *you* gonna get away? You're the one that's married."

"But you're damn near married."

"Damn near is not married." But she knew at this point there was no way she could get away from Shamari. He would be suspicious as hell, but it never hurt to dream.

"Let's go to Brazil," said Craig.

"You always hollering Brazil. What's in Brazil? You wanted to send Shamari there, so we could go to Vegas, remember?"

"Yeah, well, now I wanna go, so we can send him to Vegas."

"Where are you gonna send Anne?"

"Who?"

"Your wife, sir."

"I forgot about her."

She laughed and said, "I'm sure."

"But I wanna see you on the beach in a thong."

"It's January. It's winter."

"In Brazil, it's summer. It starts in December there."

Craig noticed a black guy across the room staring at them. This happened often when they were out. Sometimes it would be white women, other times black guys.

"Do you know the guy across the room?" He looked in the man's direction.

She turned and recognized the man immediately. Duke, Shamari's best friend, and as soon as they made eye contact, Duke approached the table.

Jada gave him a fake smile. "Hey, Duke."

"Wassup, Jada. Who's your friend?"

"Dr. Matthews. He's interviewing me for a job."

Duke extended his hand to Craig, "I'm sorry for interrupting, my man. But just look at her, you should hire her for eye candy around the office if nothing else." Duke laughed.

Craig said, "I was thinking the same thing."

Jada said, "I'll see you later, Duke. I'm sure I'll see you around."

When he left, Jada said, "Shamari's friend."

"Really?"

"Yes, the fuck really!"

"Damn."

"I know. I gotta get the fuck outta here."

"Now?"

"Fuck, yeah! There is no way I can be here with you."

"But you're on a job interview."

"Shamari knows you, man. I can't get caught here with you."

She finished her drink and left in a hurry. When she was in the car, she called Shamari, "Hey, babe. Just saw Duke."

"He told me. Said you were on a job interview. I didn't know you were looking for a job."

"You said we were broke."

"I know."

"I'll be home in twenty minutes. You want me to pick you up some lunch?"

"Just get me a turkey sandwich from Subway."

"Got ya, baby!"

CHAPTER 39

STARR'S FATHER, ACE, WAITED WITH THE BAIL BONDSMAN OUTSIDE the jail as Starr and Trey walked out.

The bondman's name was Terry. He was over six feet tall with a bald head and looked much younger than his fifty-four years. Ace had known him for twenty years. He'd been Ace's bondsman, back in the eighties, when Ace had flooded Atlanta with cocaine. Since he'd known Ace for so long, he would get anybody out of jail on Ace's word.

Trey approached Ace. "Look, man, I'm sorry that your daughter had to go through this bullshit."

Ace hugged Starr and said to Trey. "I don't understand. What happened? I saw online that you got picked up for child support. I didn't know you had children."

Starr looked furious. Knowing that her dad would find out that Trey had been fucking around on her.

Trey said, "It was a child support warrant, but, my son's mother said I had drugs in the house, so the narcotic cops came. It's a long story man."

Ace said, "I got time."

Terry the bondsman was standing there with some papers in his hand looking stupid. He finally interjected, "I need you two to sign these papers. They just say that you will appear in court."

Trey and Starr signed the papers and Terry disappeared. Trey, Starr, and Ace hopped into his old school Cadillac. Ace said, "Y'all wanna listen to some music? I got all kinds of CDs in here."

Who in the hell listened to CDs anymore, Trey wondered, but Ace was old school. He didn't look like he owned an MP3. He said, "Sure."

Ace said, "Before I pop in my CD, what the hell happened?"

Starr said, "Trey already told you that it's a long story." She sat on the passenger side of the Caddy and tried to lower the window but it was broken. Ace jumped out the car and walked to the other side, opened the door, and pushed the window down a bit, and then stuck some cardboard in between the window and the door to keep the pane from sinking into the door. The scent of the six Pine Tree air fresheners that hung from the mirror made Starr nauseous.

When he sat in the car he said, "I wanna hear."

Starr said, "I'm sure Meeka has already told you about this."

"You're sister ain't told me shit." Then he turned to Trey in the backseat. "How old are your kids?"

"Kid. It's only one. I have a son."

"How old is he."

"Five."

Ace eyebrows rose. He did the math in his head, realizing that Trey had fathered the kid during his relationship with Starr. He turned back to Trey. "I see why you don't wanna talk about it."

Trey said, "It was a mistake."

Ace threw up his hands. "I ain't judging you, brother."

Starr knew Ace was not the man to judge Trey. He'd fathered two children of his own outside of his relationship with Starr's mother.

Ace said, "But why wasn't you paying child support?"

"Man, I give that woman money every month for clothes, sports, whatever my boy needs. He even goes to private school. You know me better than that, Ace."

"But there was no record of the money you gave her?"

"No."

"Now that's where you fucked up. You should have had records of all the stuff you've done. Saved your receipts. You can't hand a woman cash and expect her to give you credit for that. I bet she probably wants to be with you too."

Ace drove the Cadillac like an eighty year old granny and it was pissing Starr off. "Can we talk about this later?" Starr interjected.

Ace slid in a CD. Rap music blared through the speakers. Six minutes later, Ace lowered the volume and said, "I'm still not understanding. Why were you locked up?"

Starr said, "Because Jessica told a goddamned lie."

"Who's Jessica?"

"My baby mama." Trey said.

Ace drove up to the driveway. Starr kissed Ace on the jaw. "Thank you, Daddy." She got out when the car stopped.

"Anything for my baby girl."

Starr disappeared into the house.

Trey stayed to chat with Ace for a few minutes.

"Boy, you fucked up. I hope you know it."

Trey sighed. "I know."

"I did that same dumb shit twenty years ago. I fathered two kids outside of my marriage and that shit still comes up to this day. Not as frequently as it used to."

Trey said, "Man, what do I need to do to make it right?"

Ace said, "There ain't shit you can do but let some time lapse. Make it all about her, but this one is going to be a hard one to get over. One thing you need to do is get that child support shit taken care of, and if I was you, I would get a restraining order against that baby mama."

"A restraining order! Come on man, it ain't that serious."

"You still screwing this woman?"

"No."

"Are you sure?" Ace looked at him with serious eyes. "Now you know you can tell me anything, I know that's my daughter, but I know a man will be a man. Hell, like I told you, I fucked up many years ago. I know what it's like to be young."

"Hell, no, Ace! I ain't lying, man. This chick just trying to make my life miserable because I'm not fucking with her."

"Well, get the restraining order. It shows my daughter that you don't wanna have shit to do with her, and your life will be a lot easier."

Trey laughed, "I ain't going through all that shit."

Ace hugged Trey and said, "Good luck." Trey strolled to the house as Ace walked to the passenger side of the car. Pulling the window up from the door, Ace folded the cardboard and slid it back between the door and window stabilizing the window again. Then he hopped back into the driver's side of the car and started it up. Rap music blasted out of the speakers as he left the plush neighborhood at a snail's pace. Old school gangster rolling.

CHAPTER 40

CHRIS AND MIKE SAT AT THE KITCHEN ISLAND COUNTER, COUNTING stacks of twenties and hundreds. Mike was running his money through a money counter and Chris was counting by hand.

Lani entered the kitchen from the garage. "Hey, baby," Chris called out.

Lani pecked Chris on the cheek and said, "Hi, Mike." She then made her way to the den.

"What's wrong, babe?" Chris said, as he banded a pile of twenties together.

Mike piled a stack of twenties in the money counter. The loud-ass money counter was annoying the hell out of Chris because he was trying to hold a conversation. Mike placed another pile of twenties in the counter.

Chris said, "Bruh, can you chill out a minute? Let me talk to Lani."

Mike said, "My bad."

Chris turned back to Lani and said, "What's wrong?"

"Nothing's wrong."

Chris smiled and said, "Now, you know I know when something is wrong. What's up?"

"How long is this bullshit going to go on between you and Black?"

"Who is Black?"

Mike laughed and said, "I knew somebody named Black, but he got murked."

"Mike, you got jokes," Lani said.

Chris stood from the table and said, "Oh, you defending that nigga? I mean this dude tried to kill me, and I'm supposed to just lay down? Really?"

"It's not about laying down. It's about having good sense."

Chris said, "Let me tell you something. I'm not letting Black or nobody else do something to me and get away."

Mike got restless and piled some more money into the counter and it began counting. When it stopped, he turned to Chris and said, "What happened to Black?" Then he laughed.

"This ain't funny. This man is in the hospital holding on to his dear life, and it's a goddamned joke to you."

"Nothing is a joke. I'm not a goddamned joke. I told you a long time ago to tell his nana to tell him to leave me the fuck alone, or else he was going to pay for all those punk-ass threats."

Lani left the room and headed upstairs. When she reached the bedroom, Chris was right behind her.

"Tell me the truth, Lani. What the fuck is up with you and Black? What is going on? I think there's more to this bullshit than you told me."

Lani was frustrated with him questioning her motives or her concern for Black. She just stared at him without answering the question. This was a question she'd answered so many times before.

Chris said, "Just as I thought. You love him."

Lani picked up the remote control from the nightstand and pointed it at the plasma TV when Chris took hold of her wrist.

Lani shoved him and said, "Will you get the fuck away from me?" She stood and elbowed him. "Motherfucker, don't ever put your goddamned hand on me!"

Chris pointed his finger in her face and said, "You're one ungrateful-ass bitch, you know that?"

"Ungrateful? What are you talking about?"

"Do I have to tell you what ungrateful means?" He laughed and said, "Maybe I do since all you got is a GED."

Lani said, "That was uncalled for"

"The truth hurts, huh."

Lani said, "And the truth is, you went to college on a basketball scholarship, flunked out, and resorted to selling weed. And you like to say you was NBA material. Motherfucker, you averaged six points a game. Nigga, I googled yo' ass."

"At least I went to college."

"And you ain't no better than me, nigga."

Lani took a deep breath. She sat back on the bed trying to calm herself down. She pointed the remote at the television again.

Chris yanked the remote out of her hand and threw it against the wall, shattering it into pieces.

Lani laughed, "You're one immature-ass motherfucker."

"What's so funny?"

"You're funny," she continued to laugh and this infuriated Chris.

He said, "Why don't you admit it? You love him?"

"I'll admit you're an insecure motherfucker."

"You know you love him."

"I'll always have love for him. I was with him for years, but you're my man now. But I'm not going take you verbally abusing me because you gave me a few trinkets."

"Trinkets?"

"You know what trinkets are, college boy!"

"I'm just tripping that you describe what I bought you as trinkets."

"I'm just saying you might call me ungrateful, but I'm used to having shit. I've always had the best."

"Courtesy of Black?"

"Courtesy of whoever. I've always had players, and I ain't talking 'bout no basketball players. Dudes with way more money than you'll ever have."

Mike burst into the room. "What the fuck is going on?"

Lani said, "You need to get your brother, Mike. I've had enough of his goddamned mouth."

Chris stood in front of her. "What you gonna do to me, Lani?"

Lani laughed and said, "I can't believe this punk-assed motherfucker is in my face like I'm a dude."

Mike grabbed Chris by the shoulder and said, "What the fuck are you doing?"

Chris said, "You know I ain't gonna hit her, bruh. She got too much mouth and she's ungrateful as hell.

Mike yanked his brother by the arm and led him out of the room.

CHAPTER 41

A WHITE BENTLEY DROVE UP TO THE DRIVEWAY. STARR YELLED, "Baby, somebody is in our driveway!"

Trey said, "Yeah, I told Shamari to come over."

Starr sighed and said, "Oh good, it's not enough that we just got out of jail, and now these nosey-ass neighbors are going to be wondering why we having people coming over our house driving fancy cars."

"Come on, there are at least twenty high-end vehicles in this neighborhood. I don't give a fuck what they think anyways!"

"But we're the only ones whose house got raided a few days ago."

"For child support," Trey said.

"It doesn't matter. All our white neighbors seen was us getting taken to jail in the early morning."

"I'm not living my life to make them happy."

Trey approached Starr and slapped her on the ass. "Quit worrying."

He opened the door.

Starr said, "Hey, Shamari."

Shamari smiled and said, "Good to see you." Then he and Trey disappeared into the den.

Trey sat on the large sofa and Shamari sat on an armchair right across from him.

Shamari said, "What's up?"

"Just got out of jail."

"What the fuck happened?"

"Baby mama apparently took me to court for child support."

"What?"

"It's a long story, but basically, she's just mad cuz I don't want her ass. Feel me?"

"Yeah, I know how that shit can be."

"And she took a warrant out on my lady for communicating a threat, so they picked us both up."

"What the fuck is wrong with her!"

"Yeah man, she's crazy. Really fuckin' crazy. Like she's a stalker type bitch."

"So any other news? Needing to know when we're going to be in power?"

"Just give me a couple of more days."

Shamari said, "Good, cuz I'm about to sell this goddamned Bentley. I gotta get my hands on some paper, bruh."

Trey said, "I might need the guy you used to get rid of those problems you had."

"What?"

"I need somebody touched."

Shamari looked confused.

"I think somebody is talking."

"Really?"

Shamari avoided Trey's eyes. "Well, the guy that I use is in jail."

"For what?"

Shamari said, "First of all, tell me what happened?"

"One of my runners got caught with ten ki's coming out of Houston."

"He's probably telling."

"Ya think?" Trey said sarcastically.

"Ten ki's will get you life."

"I know. It's a pretty bad situation to be in."

"Does he have a record?"

"I don't think so." Trey paused. "Why can't I use your guy to handle the situation?"

"He got arrested. I told you"

"For what?"

"Attempted murder. He tried to kill a federal witness and it went wrong." Shamari took a deep breath. "He was sloppy. Very sloppy, bruh."

Trey took it all in. Thinking about Shamari's enforcer being locked up for trying to take a federal snitch out, Trey knew there was no way in hell he was going to do business with this guy. He had enough problems of his own.

"Yeah it went bad. Real bad," Shamari said, avoiding Trey's eyes. Then he said, "Yeah, I didn't wanna say nothing but it went bad for me. Part of the reason I'm broke. You feel me? I had to pay lawyer fees and then I paid him for the job. Now I'm broke, but he's not going to say anything. I'll be okay."

"You sure?"

"I can never be sure that he's not going to say anything later, but right now, it's all good."

"Yeah right now it is, but what about later?"

"Can we ever be certain about anything in life?"

There was a long silence and Trey was deep in thought.

Trey said, "That's true."

Shamari said, "If you want to get somebody touched, it's better that you do it yourself. At least you know you're going to do it the right way, and you won't have to worry about it coming back to haunt you."

"You're right."

Shamari gave Trey a pound and he headed to the front door.

Starr was sitting in the living room and when they made eye contact, she said, "Bye, Shamari."

Shamari smiled and said, "Take care, Starr."

"Tell Jada I said hi." Starr said, giving him a fake smile.

"I will."

When Shamari pulled off, Starr said to Trey, "He seems like a nice guy."

"Seems cool, but that nigga's got major issues."

"What?"

"Man, I'd rather not say. I don't even want you to know the type of shit he's into. This way it will never come back to you."

Starr said, "Cool." She knew Trey well enough to know not to ask too many questions if he didn't want to tell her something.

Trey changed the subject. "How is his girl, anyway?"

"She's okay, I guess."

"What do you mean, you guess? She's your friend, ain't she?"

"How many times I gotta tell you, she is not my friend."

Trey laughed.

Starr said, "She's a ho."

Trey said, "Huh?"

"Fucking a rich white man for money."

"What?"

"And fucking him while Shamari was in jail."

"How do you know this?"

"When I left you after all your baby mama drama started, I saw her in the lobby of the W in Buckhead early one morning with a white man."

Trey said, "Okay, but that don't mean that she fucked him."

Starr said, "You're right, that don't mean they fucked, but I don't believe they were up in the room playing UNO."

"Trifling bitch," Trey said.

"Nigga, you ain't no saint yourself."

Trey wanted to say something but he knew it was best he didn't respond. He didn't need to rehash the situation about Jessica.

CHAPTER 42

TREY'S CONNECT HAD SENT HIM TWENTY KILOS OF COCAINE. THIS WAS more than enough to make up for the money he'd lost. He wanted Monte dead, but he knew that he couldn't kill him now. He'd told Shamari the plan before he knew that Shamari already had a friend locked up for the attempted murder of an informant. There was no way he could go through with Monte's execution now. He'd been in business long enough to know that if he had Monte knocked off and the Feds picked up Shamari, there was a good chance Shamari would use that information to get out of prison. Luckily, Shamari didn't know who Monte was, but there was still no way he could go through with it now. Even though Shamari seemed like a stand up guy, Trey believed enough pressure would make him crack. Since he wasn't going to kill Monte, he needed to move to a new place and move fast. Starr found a penthouse in downtown Atlanta that an African surgeon was willing to rent. It was a little over six thousand square feet, right in the heart of Buckhead, with floor to ceiling glass windows. Trey felt like he was the president looking over Atlanta.

Starr walked up behind him, "I love this place."

"Me too, we should have moved here a long time ago."

Starr said, "One thing for sure, I'm glad that Jessica bitch does not know where we're at."

Trey frowned, "Well, you know that she's going to find out."

"How the fuck is she gonna find out?"

"She has my son, remember?"

Starr was silent. She didn't like the fact that Jessica had a child by her man and she was still childless. Hearing Trey say Jessica had his son stung. She began to cry.

Trey said, "What's wrong?"

She rubbed her eyes and tried to keep from crying, but she couldn't hold back the tears.

Trey hugged her and said, "I promise I'm going to give you a baby."

Starr smiled but then said, "It's not going to be the same."

"What do you mean?"

"If I get pregnant, it won't be your first baby, so we won't be experiencing it together."

Trey said, "Look, I know I fucked up, and if I could take it back, I would." He paused then said, "Well, I won't take my son back. I love my son, but if I—"

She cut him off and wrapped her arms around him. "I know what you mean. I know exactly what you mean."

CHAPTER 43

SHAMARI STILL HAD NOT SOLD THE BENTLEY AND HAD RESORTED TO selling a few pounds of weed here and there to stay afloat. He wasn't making the kind of money he was used to making, but it was paying the bills. He was now driving a Toyota Camry and hid the Bentley in the backyard to avoid repossession. The Camry wasn't a bad ride, and in fact, he wished he'd been driving this car all along instead of squandering all his money on luxuries. He really felt like a goddamned fool because he'd had millions of dollars and now he didn't have a goddamned thing to show for it, even though he'd been hustling for fourteen years straight. Now he wished he was a regular 9-5 dude. He parked the Camry and entered the house. Jada handed him a notice from the Sheriff.

"What the fuck is this?"

"Well, it says that we have fifteen days to get the fuck out! We haven't been paying the rent. We gotta go, babe, or catch up the rent."

Shamari stared at the court order. "I ain't got no goddamned sixteen thousand dollars to give nobody."

Jada then passed Shamari a big manila envelope.

He sighed and said, "What the hell is this?"

"Just look inside, babe."

Shamari tore into the envelope and said, "What the fuck? Whose money is this?" He brandished a handful of hundred dollar bills.

"I'm giving this to you, Shamari. You've always been so good to me and my family. It's the least I can do for you."

He handed her the envelope back.

She said, "What's wrong?"

"I can't take your money. I honestly cannot take your money, baby."

"Look, we're about to get put out. Now is not the time for some stubborn-ass pride. Take the goddamned money and pay the rent."

Shamari took the envelope back and said, "I'm not going to pay the rent."

"Huh?"

"We're moving somewhere cheaper, and I'll take the money that we have and buy something to get back on our feet with."

Jada said, "What happened to Trey? I thought you two were going to do business together?"

Shamari said, "Me too, but he never called me, man. I can't be worried about what another nigga say he's going to do for me. I gotta go out there and make it happen." He set the court order down and counted the money. "Damn! This is twenty five thousand dollars. Where did you get this from?"

Jada said, "I took some of my stuff to the consignment shop when you told me we were in trouble."

"Damn! And you got twenty five thousand dollars?"

Jada said, "I still got a lot of shit I've never worn. If I need to sell some more things, I will. I'm down for you, Shamari." She hugged him.

He gripped her ass, kissed her neck, and said, "I love you baby!"

CHAPTER 44

SHAMARI FINALLY GOT TREY ON THE PHONE AND THEY AGREED TO meet at a Starbucks in Buckhead. Trey sat at a table in the corner with his feet kicked up on a table, peering out of the window. They greeted each other with a pound. Trey said, "Did you want something?"

"Naw, don't usually have lattes with gangsters."

"You got jokes."

"No jokes. Just not a Starbucks type of guy." Shamari sat across from Trey, and as soon as he was comfortable, he said, "You know what? I think I'll have a cup of coffee. Do they even have regular coffee here?"

"I'm sure."

Shamari eased up to the counter, and seconds later he was back on the sofa with a cup of black coffee.

Trey said, "No cream for your coffee."

"No cream for me." He sipped and set it on the floor.

Trey said, "Bruh, I'm gonna be honest with you. I just can't bring myself to do business with you. I think it's best that we not fuck with each other on that level."

Shamari looked confused, "What're you talking about man?"

"You're too fuckin' hot, man. I ain't gonna get caught up in your bullshit, dude. I gotta lot of shit going on of my own."

Shamari had a confused look on his face. He cracked his knuckles as his eyes roamed Starbucks. Now that he had some money to spend, he'd hoped that he and Trey could do some good business, so he could get back on his feet.

He sighed and said, "What the fuck does what I did have to do with you?"

"You tried to kill a snitch, man."

Shamari leaned forward and said, "And just the other day, you were talking about doing the same thing."

"One of your friends is downtown, right now." Trey sipped the green tea in front of him and then said, "If you don't think that dude is going to tell on you, you're out of your goddamned mind."

Shamari said, "You're hot too, motherfucker."

"Am I?"

"The driver that got bagged coming from Houston with the ten bricks, remember?"

"Now, that's exactly why we shouldn't be doing business."

Shamari stood and said, "It's all good. I knew you were a fake-ass nigga."

"What the fuck ever, clown."

Trey stood so he was nose to nose with Shamari. He wanted to slap the shit out him, but Shamari didn't look like a punk. He knew that if he slapped him, they would tear Starbucks up. Two geek-looking white dudes at a table a few feet away stopped working and started looking in their direction.

A tall, thin, redheaded manager named Jason yelled from behind the counter, "You two need to leave right now. Or I'm calling the police."

Shamari said to Trey, "You need to get the fuck out my face before I hurt you, dude."

Jason came from behind the counter with a black girl whose nametag said 'Brooke' to diffuse the situation.

Brooke whispered, "Please leave. He'll call the police. I've seen him do it too many times."

Shamari picked up his coffee that sat on the floor and eased past Trey.

"Exactly what I thought. Exactly! All bark and no bite."

Shamari said, "I ain't no goddamned pit bull, I'm a gangster."

"Dude, you need to be worried about that trifling-ass bitch of yours."

Shamari stopped in his tracks. "Huh?"

Trey said, "Yeah nigga. Ya bitch."

"What about my lady?"

"I bet she likes cream in her coffee. That's all I'm saying."

Shamari set his drink down and ran toward Trey, but Brooke wedged herself between them and said, "Please leave. Please leave."

Jason was holding up his cell phone, threatening to dial 911 as the two men left.

• • •

Shamari jumped into his Camry and was driving home as fast as he could when his phone buzzed. A text message from Trey.

That doctor that's been working on your wifey's body has really been working on her body! Take care of your home, nigga. LOL.

Trey dialed Jada's number. There was no answer. He called her three more times and the phone rang, but she didn't answer. He texted her. *'You need to call me right now'*

CHAPTER 45

CRAIG AND JADA WERE IN THE TAPIAN LOUNGE, INSIDE THE MANDARIN Oriental Hotel.

"You look amazing tonight," Craig said as he reached for Jada's thigh. Jada slapped his hand and continued to nurse a tall glass of Chardonnay.

She knew she looked great, but not amazing. The skirt she wore showed off all of her curves and she wore some extra skinny heels today. The shoes had seven inch platforms and she could barely walk in them, but they made her legs look so goddamned long and she loved that look.

Craig said, "Order some champagne."

"What's the occasion?"

"No occasion, I'm just so happy to see you."

"Really? Why?"

"I haven't seen you in—"

"Three days." She cut him off.

"The longest three days of my life."

"You missed me." She sipped her wine.

"I always miss you."

She smiled and uncrossed her legs before crossing them again, giving him a glimpse of her bare kitty. She'd gone commando on purpose. She wouldn't give him any today, but she wanted him to be aroused. She noticed that whenever she dressed sexy, he was nicer. She would leave with gifts and money. All of which she loved.

Craig said, "Why aren't I your man?"

She smiled playfully. "I have no idea what you're talking about."

"Why are you so mean to me?"

"What in the hell are you talking about?"

"Why won't you be mine?"

"You have a wife." Damn she was beginning to get annoyed at his suggestions of her becoming his mistress.

The truth was that she'd thought about what it would be like to be his mistress. She was so glad he had a wife that he had to go home to. It was easier to control the situation.

Her phone buzzed for the fifth time. She pulled it out and had a look at it. Shamari again. She excused herself and disappeared into the ladies room to call him back.

"Hello"

"Hello, my ass!"

"What's your problem?"

"You! You been fucking that goddamned plastic surgeon, haven't you?"

"What are you talking about?"

"He's Craig, that's his name," he huffed. "He's Craig, right?"

"Excuse me?"

"Answer the goddamned question, Jada Simone."

"First of all, you don't need to be calling me no goddamned Jada Simone. You're not my mama!"

"I'm ya man. Well, I thought I was your man, but I guess I got that wrong too."

"What are you talking about?"

"You know goddamned well what I'm talking about, Jada."

Jada wondered how he knew. Had he followed her to the hotel? Was he somewhere waiting on her? She had to play it cool to see exactly how much he knew.

"Jada? Are you there?"

"Yes, I'm here."

"Answer my question!"

"What question?"

"Don't play dumb, bitch!"

"What are you talking about?"

"I'm talking about the man that I've paid thousands of goddamned dollars to so your insecure ass can look like a goddamned Barbie doll."

"I'm not fucking nobody!"

"Where are you, Jada?"

Two drunk blondes burst into the bathroom. The taller of the two said to Jada, "You have an amazing ass."

Jada smiled politely but didn't say anything.

The tall blonde said to her partner, "Look at it. It's perfect, like two round balls."

Shamari said, "Where the fuck are you? I hear people around you."

"I'm out right now, Shamari." Jada ducked into a stall.

"With who?"

"I'm with Lani. We're getting some drinks then we're heading to the hospital."

"The hospital?"

"Yeah, her ex-boyfriend, Black, got shot."

"I know Black. Why haven't I heard anything about it?"

Jada said, "I don't know. I think it just happened."

"Are you fucking the doctor?"

A tear rolled down Jada's face. Her lies had caught up with her. Though she'd fucked Craig, she really didn't want to hurt Shamari. She felt so bad.

"Answer, goddamn it! Answer me, Jada!"

She didn't want to lie to him any further. She didn't want to hurt him anymore. She terminated the call and turned the phone off. She dug into her purse and removed another phone—the one that she used to keep in touch with Craig. She dialed Lani's number. She prayed that Lani would pick up the phone. She knew Lani probably hadn't saved the number. Lani picked up right away. "Hello?"

"It's me, Jada."

"I knew I recognized the number. This is your other phone, right?"

"Yeah,"

"Wassup?"

"Girl, shit done hit the fan."

"What you tombout?"

Jada sighed then said, "My man, Shamari, knows about Dr. Handsome."

"What?"

"Yeah. He knows, girl."

"How?"

"I don't know how he knows, but he knows."

"What did he say? Where are you? How did he find out?"

"Girl, I'm so goddamned scared. I don't know what to do? Where are you?"

"I'm at home."

"You need to leave cuz I told him I was out with you. Told him that we were at the hospital visiting Black."

"What?" Lani said. "Damn, now you done got me involved in your shit."

"I ain't have no choice."

"Let's meet. Somewhere."

"Okay I'm out with Craig, but I'll ditch him. Where do you wanna meet?"

"Let's meet at Onyx," said Lani.

"Okay, Onyx in thirty minutes."

"See you in thirty," said Lani.

CHAPTER 46

A STRIPPER NAMED SKYY SAT WITH JADA AT A TABLE NEAR THE MAIN stage of Club Onyx. Jada had met Skyy at a party a few years ago and they'd both gotten drunk and spent the night together. Jada was so wasted, she'd let Skyy go down on her, but whenever the question of whether she'd been with a girl came up, she would swear to God she hadn't but would like to one day. She had all but blocked the incident with Skyy out of her mind. Skyy was a pretty, light skinned woman with a very tiny waist and a huge ass with just a handful of tits. A tattoo of a scorpion covered her back. She was from Memphis and had been dancing at Onyx for the last six or seven years, dancing to support her son. Skyy was sipping a vodka and orange juice. "So what brings yo uppity ass in here?"

"Come on, Skyy. You know I come in here from time to time."

"Yeah, but I ain't seen ya in a while. What brings ya out?"

"I'm supposed to meet my girlfriend here. Girls night out, ya know?"

"Your friend or your *girlfriend?*" Skyy winked.

"Now you know I don't do girls, Skyy."

"A little birdie told me otherwise."

"Skyy, I was drunk. Remember? That shit won't happen again, so quit talking about it."

"Whatever. You know you liked it." She simulated oral sex with the straw in the glass of vodka.

"Pretending to suck a dick does nothing for me."

Skyy licked the straw. "Well, pretend this is your clit."

Jada said, "Now, when my friend comes in here, please don't bring that shit up."

Skyy said, "Buy me another drink, and you got yourself a deal."

Jada flagged a waitress who was wearing some fishnets and a black thong. The waitress barely looked twenty-one, had a pony-tail, and braces.

"Can you get her another drink?" asked Jada.

Skyy said, "You have to buy the drink for yourself and give it to me. Club rules."

Jada said, "Bring me what she has."

The juvenile-looking waitress headed to the bar for the drink just as Lani walked in and approached the table.

Jada said, "Lani, this is Skyy."

Lani and Skyy shook hands as the juvenile dropped the drink down in front of Jada who slid the drink to Skyy. Jada gave the waitress a twenty dollar bill.

A pretty brown skinned girl walked by the table. The girl and Lani locked eyes for a long time before the girl sat on Skyy's lap. Skyy grabbed her ass playfully and said, "This is my friend, Tika."

Lani and Tika locked eyes again, before Lani asked, "Where do I know you from?"

"I don't know, but you sure as hell look familiar."

"Where you from?"

"Oakland, California, baby."

"Oakland?"

"The Yay area. You know anything about the Yay area? Repping the 3-1-0. All day, every day."

"Definitely not there. I've never been there."

Tika said, "Maybe I saw you in the mall somewhere. You look familiar too."

Skyy said to Tika, "Bitch, what time you get here?"

"Thirty minutes ago." Tika stood and said, "It's dead in here, but I gotta make my rounds. Can't pay my bills just sitting here talking unless these girls want some dances."

Lani was disgusted by the thought of a girl dancing for her.

Jada said, "Not right now. Actually, Skyy, I wanna talk to my girl for a few minutes alone, if you don't mind." She removed a fifty dollar bill from her purse and passed it to Skyy.

Skyy gulped her drink down and disappeared.

Lani was still trying to remember where'd she'd seen Tika.

Jada said, "I can't go home. This motherfucker is going to kill me. He's gonna fuck me up. I know it."

"Shamari is not that fucking dumb. He ain't gonna jeopardize his freedom by hitting you."

Jada said, "He's mad as fuck."

"You don't know what he knows."

"You're right. I don't know what he knows, but the main thing is that he knows that I been fucking around with Craig."

"How'd he find out?"

"I don't know. I'm thinking he had a motherfucker follow me or something. I don't know. Honestly, I don't know what the fuck or how the fuck he got his information. All I know is that he is mad as fuck."

"Of course he is," Lani said. "I need a motherfuckin' drink."

The juvenile came back over and Lani ordered a Ciroc and coke. Jade got two shots of Patron and the juve brought them back seconds later. Lani gave her thirty dollars and she was gone.

Lani said, "Wait a minute! Am I trippin' or does our waitress look about twelve?"

The both laugh and Jada said, "I thought the same thing."

Jada gulped down one shot of Patron and said, "I can't go to that goddamned house tonight."

"Where are you going?"

"I don't know, but I ain't going there."

"You can stay at my house."

"That would be the first place he looked and the second would be my Mama's house. I think I'm going to get a room. Maybe the Four Seasons or something."

"So what did Craig say?"

"About what?"

"Did you tell him that Shamari found out about y'all?"

"I didn't tell him shit. Just told him an emergency came up, and I had to go."

"Simple as that?" Lani said as she sipped her drink.

Jada finished the second shot of Patron and the waitress bought two more.

"Slow down with that liquor."

"I got too much shit on my mind."

"You do that, but remember you gotta drive home."

"I'll be fine."

Lani stood and said, "I have to go, but I'll drop you off at the Four Seasons in Buckhead. You can leave your car here, and we'll come back tomorrow."

"No, I'm going to stay. I'll be okay"

CHAPTER 47

WHEN JADA OPENED HER EYES, THE FIRST THING SHE NOTICED WAS A pile of dirty clothes in the corner of the bedroom. The second thing she noticed was kid-scribbled crayon graffiti. Where in the fuck was she? How did she get here? Where in the hell were her panties? She heard water running behind the door that was adjacent to the bed. She sprang from the bed and opened the door. Skyy stood there, butt ass naked, brushing her teeth. When Skyy and Jada made eye contact, Skyy stopped brushing.

"How did I get here, Skyy?"

Skyy spat into the sink and gargled some water. "Girl, you was drunk as fuck last night. I couldn't let you drive home by yourself."

Jada was trying to jog her memory. She remembered being in Onyx. She remembered Lani being with her but Jada had driven to the club. "Skyy, where is my car?"

"Your car is still at the club. Out front. Don't worry, nothing is going to happen. It's in the very front of the club."

"But nobody is there. How do you know that nothing is going to happen to it?"

Skyy spit in the sink again. "See that's the thing. Somebody is there. The cleaning crew is there." She glanced at her watch. "They just left an hour ago."

"What time is it?"

"11:00"

"Goddamn it, I got to go. My man is going to kill me for staying out all night." As soon as Jada said that, it all began to come back to her. She had gone to the club to get her mind off the fact that Shamari had found out she'd been creeping with Craig.

Skyy said, "I gotta go pick my son up from his grandma's house, and then I can take you to get your car."

"Cool."

Skyy smiled and said, "You were amazing last night."

"What the hell are you talking about?"

"I didn't know you were such a passionate kisser."

"Huh?

Skyy rinsed off her toothbrush and said. "Don't worry, you didn't go down on me. I went down on you again. You were fucked up, but you're still the same selfish bitch that only wants to be pleased."

Jada massaged her temple. "Please tell me I didn't sleep with yo ass again."

Skyy rinsed her toothbrush off and grinned. "You didn't sleep with my ass again. You satisfied?" she smiled.

Jada said, "I need an Excedrin." She didn't want to dwell on what she may or may not have done with Skyy. As long as she didn't remember it, she was cool.

"I got some Tylenol on the dresser. "

Jada stepped back into the bedroom. There was a pink vibrator and a big black penis dildo lying on the dresser. She couldn't help but think of the fact that she slept with Skyy again. The only woman she'd ever slept with had gotten her twice while she was drunk. The Tylenol was sitting between the vibrator and the black penis. She picked up the bottle and dumped two tablets into the palm of her hand.

Skyy handed her a half bottle of water. "I'm sorry, this is the only water I got unless you want tap."

Jada swallowed the pills and drank the water. Then she scanned the room for her clothes before saying, "Where's my panties?"

"You didn't wear any."

"Get the fuck out of here."

"Seriously, you didn't have any on."

She was about the curse Skyy out but then remembered she'd gone commando because she was meeting with Craig.

Skyy handed Jada her clothes. They were folded neatly.

Jada said, "Thanks. I'm gonna need to shower before we head out."

CHAPTER 48

LOUISE SAID, "CHARLES, I KNOW YOU HEAR THE GODDAMNED DOORBELL ranging." She made her way through the den. Charles was passed out drunk on the sofa. Louise slapped him upside his head. "Wake yo ass up."

Charles yelled, "I don't give a damn about shit." Gibberish in his sleep that didn't mean anything, thought Louise as she opened the door. "Hey, Shamari. Bring yo yella ass in this house and gimme a hug."

Shamari came in and hugged Louise and she closed the door.

"Where is Jada Simone?"

"That's why I'm here."

"Well, come on in here and have a seat."

Shamari followed Louise to the den. Charles was asleep with one shoe on and slobbering all over the pillows.

When Louise noticed that Charles was still sleeping and hadn't done a goddamn thing, she excused herself to the kitchen and came back with a frying pan and clocked Charles across his head.

"Goddamn it, Louise," he hollered.

He sat up on the couch, holding his head.

"Motherfucker, get the hell out of here. We got company, you drunk ass," yelled Louise.

"What? Who?" Charles said, still holding his head. Then he made eye contact with Shamari.

"Jada's Simone's boyfriend, Shamari. You remember him?" said Louise.

"Hey, Shamari. How you been?" Charles smiled and revealed his brown teeth.

"Will you get the fuck out of here and let me and Shamari talk."

Shamari giggled.

Charles stood and Louise noticed a pee stain on his pants and said, "Now, I know this nigga didn't pee on my goddamned sofa."

Charles looked down and said. "That's not pee, that's beer—"

Before he could go further, Louise clocked him upside his head twice. Charles fell to his knees and Louise bitch slapped him twice more.

"Louise, I'm telling you that it's not pee, it's beer." Then he pointed to the floor. "See that stain on the floor? That's where I wasted my beer."

Louise clocked him with the frying pan one more time. "I don't give a damn if it's beer. That only means that you been dranking my beer. You ain't have no money fo' no beer, so what the fuck you dranking mine fo'."

Louise dropped the frying pan on the table and grabbed Charles by his dirty t-shirt and led him to the back door. "You get outside on the porch."

"It's forty-four degrees out there."

"I don't give a fuck." She shoved him outside and locked the door. "Teach you about dranking my goddamned beer."

Louise came back into the den. Shamari was sitting in the armchair.

"So, what do you need to talk to me about?"

"It's Jada."

"What about Jada?"

"She's been fucking around on me."

" You watch yo goddamned mouth, Shamari. You respect me and don't curse around me."

Shamari was amazed that Louise had the nerve to say this. When every other word that came out of her mouth was a curse word. But it was her house, so he would oblige.

"Well, one of my friends saw her out with a white man."

Louise said, "A white man? I don't believe that."

"It's true."

Louise gave him the side-eye, "How do you know this?"

"Well, another friend told me the same thing, and when I asked Jada had she been seeing him, she wouldn't answer me."

Louise said, "Okay, suppose it is true. What can I do about that?"

Shamari said, "I don't expect you to do anything. I was just letting you know, and I was wondering if you seen her."

"Last time I seen Jada Simone was two weeks ago. She called me the other day, but I missed the call. I called her back and she didn't pick up."

"I see."

"Shamari, you know me and Jada ain't that close, but we're trying."

"I know. It must be hard for you."

"Well, I just want her to forgive me. I know I haven't been the best mama."

"Can you do me a favor?"

"What?"

"Call her. She'll pick up for you."

There was a loud knock at the door. Then Charles yelled. "Louise, can you at least give me my shoes. I'm freezing my ass off out here."

Shamari chuckled and said, "Will you do me that favor?"

"I'm not doing that, Shamari. What's between you and Jada is between you and Jada. What I look like, betraying my own daughter? Look, I'm sorry you're going through this, but I can't help you."

Shamari said, "All I wanna do is talk to her. I wanna know why she did what she did. Look, I don't wanna hurt nobody, but your daughter has hurt the fuck outta me. She's broken my heart, and I feel like hurtin' somebody."

Louise stood up and disappeared into the back room. She came back with a shotgun. "Shamari, I'm gonna tell yo yella ass one time and one time only. If you touch Jada Simone, yo mama is gonna be burying you. You better let it go. As a matter a fact," Louise aimed the gun at Shamari, "you get the fuck up and get out of my goddamned house."

Shamari was slow standing, but once he was on his feet he held his hands up and said, "So, it like that?"

"Damn right it's like that. You talking about hurting one of mine. Nigga, you better ask somebody about Louise. I don't play no motherfuckin' games. Now get the fuck outta here before I shoot you in yo ass."

Shamari walked over to the door and opened the door. Charles was standing outside rubbing his bare foot with his sock-covered foot in a futile attempt to warm it.

Louis said, "Charles, get yo dumb ass in this house."

Charles slipped past Shamari, who had his eyes on Louise and the shotgun. Louise said, "I swear to you, if you touch my goddamned daughter, I will kill you."

Shamari said, "You have a good day too, Louise."

Louise fired a shot over Shamari's head making him run to his car and drive away as fast as he could.

CHAPTER 49

WHEN LANI ENTERED BLACK'S HOSPITAL ROOM, SHE SAW BLACK WAS wide awake talking to Nana. He grinned when he saw Lani and said, "I knew my wife was coming to see me."

Lani couldn't help but smile. She was glad to see Black doing well.

Nana said, "I'm so glad you came to see him. You're all he's been talking about. Well, you and his kids. And they've *all* been up here."

Black said, "Come over and gimme a hug."

Lani leaned over to give him a hug and Black put his hand on her ass.

Nana said, "Tyrann, quit being disrespectful."

Black grinned, "Oh my bad, Nana."

Lani said, "Same ole' Black."

"I missed you babe."

"Well, you know I was coming to see you. I care about you."

Black said, "You love me. Why don't you just admit it."

"I got love for you."

Nana said, "I've always told him that you were the best girl he ever had."

Lani sat on the other side of the room and said, "Too bad he didn't know that when he had me."

"I did," said Black

Nana said, "Tyrann, you know I love you, but you treated this woman like shit, and that's why you got what you deserved."

Black looked confused. "Nana, you trying to say I deserved to get shot."

"I'm not saying that at all. I'm saying Lani deserves to be happy even if it's not with you. You had your chance and you blew it."

Black said, "She's gonna be my wife. She don't know it yet, but I'm getting my woman back."

Nana said, "Im'ma go down to the cafeteria, so you two can have a moment alone."

When Nana was gone, Black said, "How you been?"

Lani said, "I've been good. I was worried about you."

"I'm gonna be okay. Doctor said I should recover fully. There's a bullet in my back that they don't wanna take out. Said if they moved it, I might be paralyzed, and one of my kidneys is gone, but I'll be okay."

"Really? You think that's okay?"

Black smiled and said, "Look, when you done as much shit as I've done on the streets, you gotta consider this a blessing. The good Lord could have taken me away, and it would've been completely justified. I'm nobody's angel."

Lani said, "I guess if you look at it that way, you're right."

Black said, "I'm blessed."

"You sure are."

"But I'm gonna get that nigga, Chris."

Lani eased back over to the bed. "Listen, please let this rest. Somebody is gonna get killed the next time."

She and Black locked eyes and he said, "Nobody has ever did nothing like this to me and got away it."

"You just said yourself you could have been killed."

"But they didn't kill me. That's the difference between them and me. I can't let this ride. Somebody has to pay."

She noticed a part on the side of his dreadlocks. "What happened here?"

"They cut my hair. Bullet fragments in my head."

"Damn! And you wanna keep this shit up?"

"Hey, it's all I know."

"I think you should let it go. You got four kids and a grandma depending on you."

"And my kids would've been without a father had them niggas succeeded."

"But, Black, you started it. You did all this bullshit because you wanna be with me."

"I do wanna be with you."

"Black this is crazy! Beyond excessive. You're a fucking mad man."

He squinted and said, "Damn it."

"What's wrong?"

"My fucking leg is in pain. Can you push the button over my head for the nurse?" he asked.

She pressed it.

Black said, "Look, I fucked up when we were together, but we were a team. You know everything about me and I know everything about you."

"So that means we're supposed to be together?"

"No, it means we come from the same place."

"What place is that?"

"The ghetto."

"I need to be with somebody from the ghetto?"

"You need to be with somebody that knows you. Somebody that you don't have to be fake around, and I'm that person."

The nurse came in. A fat brunette by the name of Meredith.

Meredith's smile said she had a nice demeanor. "Hey honey," she said in a very country accent."

Black said, "I'm in pain."

"Where is the pain coming from?"

"Mainly my leg, but my shoulder hurts too."

"Okay, I'll let the doctor know. And meantime, can I get you anything to eat? Some food or a soda?"

Black said, "Dr. Pepper."

Meredith left and came back with the soda and was gone again.

Black popped open the can of soda and said, "I want to be with you."

"But you're going about it the wrong way."

"You telling me I got a chance."

There was a long pause. She didn't know how to answer the question. Though deep in her heart, she always felt that there was a chance of them getting back together.

Black said, "Look, I know I let my pride lead me to this point. I mean once I officially became his enemy, there was no turning back. You know me—I only got one speed."

"I need you to let this go. I don't wanna see nobody get killed."

Black said, "You asking me to do a lot. My reputation is on the line."

"Black, you're too old to be worrying about a reputation. You got a bullet in your back and only one kidney. Can you just chill?"

Meredith came back in with an older black doctor. "Nurse tells me you're in pain."

"Yeah."

"Leg?"

"Yup."

"Well you're scheduled for surgery in the morning. We're going to remove that bullet from your leg and it should feel much better then, but we'll give you some more pain pills for now."

Black guzzled the rest of the soda down and Lani walked over to the edge of the bed giving him a kiss on the forehead before heading toward the room door. Before she left the room, Black said, "I love you."

She turned and smiled and though she wanted to respond, she didn't.

CHAPTER 50

JADA'S PHONE RANG. IT WAS LOUISE, HER MOTHER. SHE ANSWERED it on the first ring. "Hey, Ma."

Louise said, "What the fuck is going on?"

"What are you talking about?"

"That yella-ass Shamari been over here tombout he looking for you and said somebody gonna get hurt."

"When?"

"He just left. I went grabbed my shotgun and pointed it at his ass. I told him, 'Nigga, if anybody gets hurt, it's gonna be yo punk ass cuz if you touch my goddamned daughter, yo mama gone be burying yo ass befo' sundown.'"

Jada giggled. She needed that laugh from her mama right now. She knew that eventually she would have to face Shamari and be honest about the whole situation.

"What did he say then?"

"He didn't say shit. I walked his ass right out of my house. Fired a shot over his head. You should've seen that nigga screeching out of the driveway."

"Did he say where he was going?"

"No."

"What did he tell you?"

"Something about your running around on him with some white *man*."

Jada was embarrassed even though it was true. She'd wish Shamari hadn't put her mom in her business.

Louise said, "Jada Simone, though we've had our share of run-ins, you belong to me. You came from me, and if that nigga, or any nigga, put his hands on you, they're going to answer to me. I mean it."

"Mama, don't worry about it. I'm going to handle the situation."

"You sure? If you need me, you just let me know."

"Don't worry about me. I'm going to be okay."

"You sure?"

"I'm positive."

"Jada?"

"Yeah, ma?"

"Did you fuck around on Shamari?"

There was a long pause. Jada didn't know how to answer—she didn't want to answer the question.

Louise finally said, "Jada, that wasn't right. That wasn't right at all. You know I've slept with my share of men."

Jada took a deep breath. The conversation had really become uncomfortable.

Louise continued, "A lot of people look at me and think I'm nothing but a goddamned drunk. But I'm loyal, and there was never a time when I was out selling ass that I had a man at home to answer to. Whenever I fucked a man for money, I was always single. I was always loyal to one man."

"I hear you, Mama, and I am loyal. I love Shamari. I don't know how I got myself into this."

"Nobody is perfect. But you need to meet up with this man and tell 'im how you feel.

"I will."

"I love you."

"I love you to Ma." When she hung up the phone, Skyy was beeping on the other end. "Hello?"

"Girl, you left your phone."

"What the fuck are you talking about? I'm on my phone."

"I found a white cell phone under my bed. Some motherfucker named Craig been blowing it up."

It was her other phone. She needed it. "Can you meet me at the Waffle House on Old National?"

"There's two on Old National."

"The College Park one."

"Okay. It'll take me twenty-five minutes to get there. How long will it take you?"

"I'm like ten minutes away."

"See you in a bit." She ended the call.

CHAPTER 51

AFTER JADA PICKED UP THE PHONE FROM SKYY, SHE CALLED CRAIG and told him she needed to see him right away. He agreed to meet her right after he finished a liposuction procedure at 3:00 pm. They met at the Atlanta Fish Market. He hugged her and said, "What's wrong? Did yo nigga get picked up by the police again?"

She placed the tip of her finger on his nose and said, "Motherfucker, I say nigga. You don't have the right to say it."

"I'm joking. It's slang."

"Slang that you better damn well not use!"

He grabbed her hand and held it for a while. "What's wrong, baby? Tell me what's wrong?"

She stared at him, wondering how he knew something was wrong.

"Menstrual cycle?"

"Hell, no! Craig, you did just say the word nigga. A word I'd never thought I'd hear you say."

His face became sad. "I know and I apologize. I shouldn't have said it. It was a very poor attempt at humor, but something else is wrong. You have yesterday's clothes on, and you left yesterday without giving me any kind of warning. I was thinking it must be some sort of an emergency. Why did you leave so fast?"

"Look, Craig, Shamari knows I've been seeing you, and he ain't happy."

Craig looked concerned. His blue eyes were intense. The last fucking thing he needed was some ghetto-ass drug dealer out to kill his ass. He would have to go get a firearm. How would he explain it to his wife if this was to get out? He didn't want it to get out, but he didn't want to stop seeing Jada either.

"What? How? How in the hell did this happen?"

"I don't know, but he knows."

"What do you mean, you don't know?"

"Well, he called me when you and I were together, and he kept asking me to be truthful with him about the relationship."

"What did you say?"

"I didn't answer him. I hung up the phone. I haven't seen him yet."

"Nobody knows for sure that we've been with each other," said Craig.

"His friend Duke saw us the other day."

"Yeah, but hell, he couldn't draw a conclusion from that."

Jada thought for a moment. Craig was right. How did Shamari come up with that conclusion? She remembered Starr had seen her with Craig about a month ago. Now Shamari was doing business with Trey. This shit is coming from Starr or Trey.

"So, what are you going to do?"

"I need your help now. I don't think I can live with that man again. I have nowhere to go."

"You can always go back to the townhouse."

Jada said, "I'm going to need to go there for a while. Gotta get my thoughts together."

He handed her the keys and the gate FOB.

"Thanks," Jada said

CHAPTER 52

IT WAS 3:00 AM IN THE MORNING AND LANI WAS LYING IN THE BED next to Chris when his cell phone buzzed. She hopped up to see who in the fuck was calling him at this time of morning. She picked up the phone and saw there was a text from a nigga named Sonny. She'd never heard him talk about nobody named Sonny. His phone was unlocked so she read the text.

The text said: 'I really missed you baby. I'm sorry for how I've been treating you lately.'

Lani froze. What the fuck was happening. Her man received a text from a guy named Sonny talking about how he was really sorry for how he had been treating him lately. Was Chris gay? He couldn't be. But this was Atlanta and a lot of this kind of shit had been going on. She read more texts.

Chris: Good morning.

Sonny: Good morning baby.

Chris: I'm still thinking about last night. You were off the chain."

Sonny: Blushing, I do my best. ????

Chris: When am I gonna get to see you again?

Sonny: When do you want to see me?

Chris : You know I always want to see my boo.

Lani couldn't believe what she was reading. These two niggas were going back and forth like they were in love.

Lani couldn't take it any longer. "Chris, wake the fuck up."

He didn't budge. She shook him until he finally awoke. "What the fuck is going on?"

"You tell me what's going on?" she demanded.

"What the fuck are you talking about?"

"Who the hell is Sonny?"

"Huh?"

She showed him the phone. "Some motherfucker named Sonny just texted you."

"Oh that's my homeboy!"

"I ain't never heard about him"

"You don't know all my homies."

"Apparently you don't want me to know this one. Texting this motherfucker like he's a girl or something. Telling him he was off the chain last night."

Chris became angry. "What the fuck are you doing going through my phone?"

"I'm your goddamned girlfriend, remember? If somebody text my man late at night, I'm going to find out what the fuck is going on."

"Nothing is going on."

"Oh, nothing is going on except my man likes the same thing I like."

"Hell, no," he laughed. "I'm not gay. That's the funniest shit I heard all day."

Lani said, "I'm sick to my goddamned stomach right now. Dude, you're flirting with a nigga via text. What do you call that?"

There was a long silence. Chris was trying to think of what to say next.

Lani said, "So are you a top or a bottom?"

"A top or a bottom?"

"Do you like to be on the top or the bottom?"

"Neither, I'm neither."

Lani took a deep breath. "You told your homeboy he was off the chain." She laughed and said, "You're words, not mine."

She held the phone and read another text: *I always wanna see my boo.*

He reached for the phone but she shielded him with her other hand. They struggled a bit until he took hold of her wrist. He squeezed her wrist so hard he was cutting off the blood circulation.

He said, "Drop the goddamned phone."

She held on to the phone as long as she could. Finally, she dropped the phone and covered it with her foot, so he still couldn't get to it."

"Why do you want the phone so bad?"

"Because it's my goddamned phone."

"Afraid I'm going to tell everybody your secret?"

"What secret?"

"You like niggas."

He shoved her, knocking her on her ass. She bounced up and slapped the fuck out of his bare back.

With the phone in his possession, he said, "I hate to do this to you, but there is no way in the hell I'm going to let you call me gay."

She laughed, "Go ahead and smash the phone, delete the pics, whatever you wanna do to get rid of the text, you do it. Still doesn't take away the fact that I saw them. Big time dope-boy taking it up the ass."

"I ain't deleting shit."

She said, "I think you're a bottom. You act like a bottom."

He sat down on the floor beside her and said. "You wanna know who Sonny is. Just wait. He texted Sonny: *Send me a pic, babe.*

Three minutes later a picture arrived of a woman in a red thong. Lani recognized the face. The woman from the strip club. Now it was all coming back to her. The woman at the strip club, Tika, was also the woman that was supposed to be Chris's cousin. He had said her name was Cassie, his cousin from up north. The bitch that had been by his hospital bed day and night.

Lani slapped the hell out of Chris and threw a combination of punches which connected to his chest and back. He dropped his phone and pinned her hands down to the floor. "Look, I'm sorry."

"Let me go, Chris."

"I'm sorry you had to see this, but there was no way in hell I was going to let you or nobody else think I was gay."

"Will you let me go?"

He released her hands and when they were back on their feet, she began to cry. She grabbed her pillow and headed to the guest room. He followed her.

"So you're not going to talk to me?"

"Chris, get out my face." Lani lay down on the guest bed.

Chris said, "Bitch, you can get the fuck out of my house since you wanna act like that."

Lani bounced from the bed and said, "Motherfucker, I'll go. I will get my shit and leave this tiny-ass house you think is a mansion."

"It is a mansion compared to what the fuck you grew up in."

"You know what a mansion is? Black lives in a motherfuckin' mansion and not some two-bit ass cottage like this."

She knew the mention of Black would make him rage. He ran back into the bedroom, grabbed a handful of her clothes, and flung them down the stairs.

She slid into a pair of sweatpants and sneakers and was about to leave the house when she heard him on the phone in the other room. "Yeah, I want you to come over, baby! I just kicked that bird to the curb."

Lani slammed the door so goddamned hard the window shattered. She got into her BMW and sped off.

CHAPTER 53

MONTE HAD LEFT HIS NUMBER ON A PIECE OF PAPER AND STUCK IT IN the mailbox at Trey's old house. Trey didn't want to call him, since he decided that killing him was no longer an option. He didn't know if Monte was snitching already, but Trey damn sure didn't want to give Monte a reason to snitch. So Trey would continue to pay his legal fees and even though he didn't want to give him any more money, he would have to meet him somewhere. Monte answered on the second ring. "Hello"

"Monte."

"Hey, Trey, what's up? Where you been? I been trying my best to get in touch with you. I went by your house but the neighbors said you'd moved."

"Yeah I moved. Had to leave."

"Said the police raided your house."

"Yeah, it was some child support bullshit."

"Neighbors said it was a drug raid."

"Well, my baby momma told them I was a drug dealer. I'm sure, and there were vice officers there." Trey took a deep breath and said, "Enough about that bullshit, when can I meet up with you?"

Monte laughed and said, "Hell, we can meet up right now. It's not like I got a job. Where you living? I can come over your house if you like?"

There was no way in hell Trey was going to let this clown come to his house. Not with a pending case. He didn't know if Monte had snitched, but there was no way to tell that he hadn't.

Monte said, "I can get my mama's car and come to you."

"Where does your mama live?"

"Man, you know my mama live in College Park. You've been to her house before."

"Oh, I didn't know she still lived there."

"Where else she gonna go? We ain't got money like you."

Trey thought, what the fuck was that supposed to mean? Trey sensed Monte was resenting him for having money.

"Meet me at Kroger in College Park."

Monte said, "That's five minutes away."

"I will need about an hour before I can see you. I have some other things to do."

Monte said. "Cool. I'll be driving a 2000 Buick LeSabre

"Alright."

CHAPTER 54

MONTE AND TREY PULLED INTO THE KROGER PARKING LOT AT THE same time. A blue Camaro sped by Trey. The car was going unusually fast in a parking lot pull of pedestrians. This made Trey notice two white men wearing dark sunglasses in the car.

Trey scanned the parking lot to see two more white men in the back of the parking lot in an unmarked car. What in the hell was going on? He was only there to give Monte some money. Was Monte trying to set him up? Monte called Trey. "Hello," said Trey.

"Is that you behind me?"

"Yeah."

"Did you see them idiots drive by like a bat out of hell?" asked Monte.

"Bruh, that was the police," said Trey.

"What?"

"I'm gone man. I'll see you later."

"Where are you going?" asked Monte.

Trey terminated the call and drove home. Monte called him several more times, but Trey didn't answer. Even though he knew he didn't have any product, he knew a conversation about the drug bust in Houston was all the cops needed to involve him. There was no way he was going to take a chance of getting set up by Monte. It all seemed kind of strange to him. First, the two white men speeding through the parking lot. This was College Park. He'd been in Atlanta all of his life and rarely saw white people at predominately black grocery stores. Plus, the undercover cops sitting in the parking lot, waiting on something to happen was definitely trouble.

His phone rang again. Monte again. He sent him to voicemail again.

CHAPTER 55

STARR WAS BUTT NAKED WHEN HE OPENED THE DOOR. SHE ATTEMPTED to hug him, but he pushed her hands away.

"What's wrong?"

Trey whisked right past her and stood at the floor to ceiling window overlooking the city of Atlanta. He could see Phillips Arena.

Starr eased up behind him and wrapped her arms around him. She could feel his heart pounding. "What's wrong, babe?"

"I think Monte was trying to set me up!"

"How?"

"Well I went to meet him at Kroger's in College Park, and there were police all over the goddamned place."

"I'm not understanding. Monte is the runner, right?"

"Yeah."

"Still don't get it."

"He got busted coming out of Houston."

"I had no idea."

"Well, I try not to bother you with shit like that. I don't want you to worry."

"When did he get busted?"

"Well, it was a few days before we saw him at the mall."

Starr released Trey and then disappeared into the back room to get her bathrobe. There was no sense in walking around butt naked since the possibility of getting some dick was slim.

Star said, "I'm not following tho, babe."

Trey turned to face her. "He tried to set me up."

"How? He's the freaking driver. Not like you were going to give him work."

"Right, but I was going to give him some money." Trey's face became serious. "The way it works is that if I engage in a conversation about drugs or what happened in Houston, I could get fucked. That's conspiracy."

Starr said, "I know you got his bitch-ass out of jail. Why would he do that to you?"

Trey laughed. "You know why. He don't want to go to prison for a long time. Nobody wants to go to prison."

"You were going to give him money?"

"Yeah."

Starr looked confused at first. Then she was deep in thought. "Then," she said, "I don't believe he was going to set you up, babe."

"You don't know what the fuck you're talking about!"

Her face became angry. She sat on a sectional and flicked on the TV. Scandal was on.

Trey noticed she was upset and he said, "I'm sorry, babe."

Starr said, "I know you're going through something right now, but don't fuckin' curse me because I'm here waiting on your ass to get home thinking I'm going to get some dick and you come in all upset."

Trey said, "So all you thinking about is you getting some dick?"

"Hell, no, Trey! That's not what I'm saying at all."

"What the fuck are you saying?"

"Okay, now there you go with that cursing again."

Trey eased over and stood behind the sectional and placed his hands on her shoulders and began to massage her neck.

"I'm sorry, babe."

Starr said, "It's not your fault. I know you're going through a lot."

"I am."

Starr said, "But seriously, I don't think he's trying to set you up. First of all, you're talking about a hood-ass grocery store. Trust me, something else was going on."

Trey said, "How can you be so sure?"

"Since you had something to give him, I don't think that would be the time for him to set you up. In other words, he needs that money. Now if he said he wanted to meet and there was no money involved, that would be a different story. Then I would be like, he tried to set you up."

Trey said, "Good point." He sat on the sofa and kicked off his shoes. He removed Starr's robe and placed his mouth on her nipples.

They'd dozed off after sex. She lay in his arms and he was lying there with his hand on his crotch for no good reason. The TV was watching them. Trey heard the news anchor say, "Major drug bust in the Kroger parking lot in College Park." The reporter went on to say that there were two Hispanic men trying to sell twenty-one kilos of coke to an undercover officer in the parking lot of the Kroger's in College Park. Trey sat up on the bed and used his cell phone to turn the volume up on the television. Trey saw the two men handcuffed, standing beside the blue Camaro that he had seen dash through the parking lot. He laughed then smiled. Starr had been right. He wanted to wake her and tell her but he knew that there would be hell to pay if he attempted to wake her. He thought about calling Monte, but decided he would call him in the morning. He checked his phone and noticed he'd missed two calls from Shamari and there was a text message: *Bruh, I don't want anything from you, but I would like to meet up with you, so you can tell me all that you know about Jada and the white dude.*

Though he felt bad for Shamari, he didn't respond. There was no doubt in Trey's mind that it was just a matter of time before Shamari's hit man ratted him, and he didn't want no part of that dude.

CHAPTER 56

SHAMARI'S FRIEND, DUKE, SAT PLAYING WORDS WITH FRIENDS ON his cell phone. Shamari counted the money Jada had given him days earlier. The twenty-five grand was now eighteen five. He'd had to pay a few bills and had yet to sell the Bentley.

Duke said, "Dude, forget about that bitch. She's gone and there is nothing you can do about it. I mean you were too good for her anyway. Get your mind off her. We need to make some money."

Shamari said, "I haven't said one word about her. What the hell are you talking about?"

"You've been walking around with this blank look on your face ever since this shit happened. You know I know you, bruh. I know when something is bothering you."

Shamari said, "The only thing that's bothering me is that I've never been this motherfuckin' broke in my life. That's the only thing that I'm worried about."

Duke smashed the table hard and shouted, "Motherfuck!"

"What the hell is wrong with you?"

"This chick, Tenish05, beat me again at *Words With Friends*. I know this bitch is cheating."

"If you smash my goddamned table again, I'm gonna beat you, and it ain't gonna be no goddamned game."

"Dude, you worried about the table?"

"I ain't got the money to buy a new one."

"So you're really broke?"

"No, motherfucker, I'm just pretending to be broke."

"That's what I believe."

"I don't give a fuck what you believe. The fact of the matter is that I'm broke."

There was a long silence. Duke closed the *Words with Friends* app on his cell phone.

Shamari said. "This is all the money I got to my name, and Jada gave me this."

"How much did she give you?"

"Twenty-five stacks, but I had to pay some bills."

"So the bitch is good for something."

Shamari turned his gaze away. He could feel his eyes getting moist just thinking about Jada and the last thing he needed was Duke to think he was crying over a chick.

"I've never had a woman give me money. Not even if I needed it."

"That's why it was so fucking disappointing that she did what she did because she was a down-ass chick, but I couldn't understand why she couldn't be faithful. I need answers."

"Why?"

"Why what?"

"Why do you need answers to why she did what she did?"

"Closure, I guess"

"They say women like closure. I guess men like it too."

"Well, I don't know about all men, but if you've been with somebody as long as I been with Jada, you'd wanna know what happened."

Duke stood up from the table, opened the fridge, and looked for some water. The fridge was empty. He grabbed a cup from the cabinet, dumped some ice into it, and ran some tap water.

Duke drank some water while Shamari was still trying to figure out what had happened to him and Jada. How did the relationship get to this point? It was a goddamned shame that he couldn't get the answers that he needed.

Duke said, "I have a cousin that lives off Bankhead that has weight."

"What's his prices like?"

"You mean, what's *her* prices?"

"What?"

"Dyke-bitch, but she handles her business."

"I don't fuck with girls, bruh. I don't do business with them."

"I can see her. You don't even have to see her," Duke said. He'd finished his water and was now crunching the ice. By the look on Shamari's face, it was annoying the fuck out of him.

"Bruh, this is all the money I got to my name. Do you think I'm going to give it to you to get robbed?"

"Okay. Well, you can sit here and let your money dwindle away then. I was just offering my assistance."

"Tell your cousin to give you the coke, and then I give you the money."

Duke was deep in thought. He powered his cell phone back up as he continued to crunch on the mouthful of ice until Shamari said, "Will you quit chewing on that goddamned ice?"

Duke swallowed the ice and said, "My bad."

He dialed his cousin's number. Candace picked up on the first ring. "Yeah."

"This Duke. You 'member my homie I was telling you bout? Well, we need some work. You holding?"

"Cuzzo, I told you about how to talk on them jacks. You so goddamned country."

"My bad. Can we meet somewhere? I need to talk to you."

"I'm gonna call you in a few minutes from my girl's phone. Answer."

Ten minutes later Candace called Duke. "Hello?" said Duke.

"Cuzzo, it's me."

"Yeah."

"How much money you got?"

"18 stacks."

"It's a stack an oz," Candace said.

Now Candace was talking reckless over the phone, but Duke guessed that it was a prepaid that she'd just bought. Maybe it was. Maybe it wasn't. She had the drugs. So she called the shots.

Duke turned to Shamari, "It's a stack an ounce."

Shamari said, "That's high as fuck, but I don't have a choice. Is it pure?" He wasn't used to paying that much from the Mexicans. Even Trey had better prices than this. But since he didn't have a connection, he wasn't in a position to argue.

Candace must have heard him because she said, "Tell him it's the best shit in the A."

Shamari said, "Where can we meet you?"

Candace said, "Put your friend on the phone."

Duke passed Shamari the phone. Shamari really didn't want to talk over the phone. He told Duke to put her on speaker-phone and Duke obliged

"What's up?"

Duke said, "Cuzzo, you on speaker phone."

"Cuzzo told you I only deal with the pure shit man. I'm telling you it's the best in Atlanta."

Shamari still didn't want to talk to her, so he whispered to Duke, "Everybody says that."

Candace laughed, "Look, give me the money for the eighteen, and I'll give you the rest on ya face."

"I don't wanna owe nobody no money. I just wanna get what I pay for," Shamari said to Duke.

Duke said into the phone, "We just want the eighteen."

"Okay cool, but you're gonna be calling me back."

Shamari thought it was strange that this bitch didn't care what she was saying over her phone.

Candace said, "So, where do you wanna meet?"

Duke said, "Let's meet at Auntie Helen's house in Stone Mountain."

Candace said, "Auntie Helen is out of town. I could meet him at Kroger's in College Park.

Duke said, "Fuck no! I just saw some Esse's get busted at that Kroger's. That place is hot as hell."

Candace said, "I have to go to Candler Road. Let's meet at South Dekalb Mall."

Duke looked at Shamari who nodded. "Give us about an hour," said Duke.

Candace said, "Perfect."

Shamari was counting his money again just to make sure it was right when his phone rang. Jada. He answered on the first ring. "Hey, we need to talk," said Jada.

Shamari said, "Damn right, we need to talk."

"Where are you?"

"I'm at home. Where the fuck are you?"

"Look, I'll be there in about an hour."

"Okay, I'll be waiting."

When Shamari ended the call, he said to Duke, "Call your cousin. Tell her that we're going to need a few hours."

"Why what's up?"

"I gotta get this shit straight with Jada. This bitch is going to get the fuck out of my house today. I mean right the fuck now."

Duke called Candace. "We're going to need to wait a few hours."

"Why? What's wrong?"

"Nothing, my boy just got some business he gotta take care of with his old lady. Feel me?"

"Yeah, okay. Just hit me up when you're ready."

Duke said, "For sho." Then he ended the call.

Shamari said, "Just give me a few hours then come back over. I gotta get to the bottom of this."

Duke said, "Bruh, don't do nothing crazy! As a matter of fact, you shouldn't even ask her questions you already know the answer to. She's not going to answer the questions the way you want her to. You're only going to get angrier with her."

Shamari said, "You're right, but I have to know what went wrong? How long this shit has been going on? I gotta get to the bottom of this."

Duke said, "And when you know the truth, is it going to make you feel any better?"

"No, but that's not what this is all about."

"What is it about?"

"Look, man, I don't have to answer all of your goddamned questions."

Duke said, "True, but how many times have I been with you, and you've fucked other bitches."

"Your point?"

"My point is, yeah she fucked up and she cheated, but don't be getting all self-righteous, nigga. We all have done dirt."

"I hope you're not saying that I should take this bitch back."

"No. Not at all, but don't do nothing stupid, bruh. This girl knows way too much about your business."

"True."

Duke and Shamari walked into the living room area and Shamari let Duke out the front door "I'll see you later, bruh," said Duke.

CHAPTER 57

JADA BARGED INTO THE HOUSE WEARING A PAIR OF BLACK LEGGINGS, a designer blouse which exposed a hint of cleavage and huge Jackie-O sunglasses. Jada looked damn good and even though Shamari's dick became rock solid when he laid eyes on her, she'd never find out. Wearing all new clothing that another man had purchased. The nerve of that bitch! She sat on the sofa and he sat on an armchair across from her. They stared at each other for about five minutes before she finally said, "I thought you wanted to talk to me so badly. Now that I'm here, you ain't got shit to say?"

"You're right, I don't know what to say."

There was another two-minute pause and she said. "Well I'm going to get something to drink."

"There ain't shit in here to drink. No bottled water. Nothing."

"When I left there was some Riesling in the fridge."

"Oh yeah, it's still there."

She headed to the kitchen and he knew he shouldn't be thinking about sex but those leggings made her ass look so amazing. He thought about the doctor fucking her from behind. He wondered if she had rode his dick reverse cowboy. Did she like him to call her names like slut, whore, and bitch the way she liked Shamari to do? Did she suck his dick? Did she hum on his balls? These thoughts were driving him mad. Seconds later Jada came back with some Riesling in a champagne flute.

She sat across from him with the wine glass in her hand and the ridiculous-ass Jackie-O glasses on her face. He wanted to laugh. Who the fuck did she think she was, Halle Berry? Or maybe she thought she was white since she was fucking a white man.

"So tell me, Jada?"

She sipped from her wine glass. "Tell you what?"

"How long you been fucking this man?"

"What you tombout?"

"Don't play stupid, bitch."

"Look, it's not what you think?"

"You don't know what I think."

"You're right. I don't know what you think."

"I think you've been spending a lot of time with him."

"Not a lot."

"He's been giving you gifts?"

"Sometimes."

"For sex."

"Gifts for sex is prostitution."

"I know how much you like money."

"Doesn't mean I would fuck for things. If I fucked around on you, it would be because I wanted to fuck around, not because I could be bought."

Jada just couldn't bring herself to admit to cheating on Shamari even though it was obvious that she'd been fucking around with the doctor.

"What were you doing with this man?"

She set the champagne flute on a coaster that was on the table.

Shamari said, "Will you take those stupid-ass glasses off. I wanna look you in the eye."

She removed the glasses and set them on the table beside the coaster.

"Why, Jada?"

"Why what?"

"Why the motherfuckin' disloyalty?"

Jada said, "Look, we've been going through a tough time lately, and I just needed somebody to confide in."

Shamari laughed. "Am I supposed to believe that you confided in a doctor about me. This man don't know a motherfuckin' thing about me and the life I've led. You mean to tell me, you been telling him my goddamned business. You've been telling a white man that I'm a dope dealer. You might as well go and tell the Feds."

"I haven't told him shit about you, but he knows, Shamari. He's not stupid!"

"What the hell do you mean, he knows?"

"I've had procedures with the man and each time we paid in cash. Anybody with half a brain could figure that out."

"Ok, but that's not the point. I don't give a fuck if I paid with cash or not. At what point did y'all become motherfuckin' friends?"

"After I got my boobs done, I came back six weeks later for a checkup and he suggested that we meet for coffee."

"And you met him?"

"I did."

"A married man. You met a married man for coffee. Bitch, you don't even drink coffee. What the hell?" Shamari shook his head in disgust. He couldn't believe what the fuck he was hearing.

She picked up the champagne flute again, took a quick sip and put her glasses back on. She wasn't trying to be cool, but she could feel herself getting emotional and she didn't want him to see her cry.

Shamari stood and said, "I'm not liking what I'm hearing at all. You're nothing. You never cared about me. All you ever thought about was what you can get out of me. Now it has come to this."

"Come to what?"

"Come to us ending like this. I wouldn't have never thought we would end like this."

Jada said, "It don't have to end."

"Do you think I'll take you back after what you've put me through? You're used goods."

She stood and flung the champagne flute at him, gashing him right under the eye. Blood oozed out like a waterfall. He rushed her and grabbed her around the neck. She kicked him in the balls, and he plummeted to the floor. She dashed outside and was heading for her car.

Shamari made his way to the bedroom, grabbed a handful of her clothes that she hadn't ever worn, and sprinted to the front door. Just when she was about to back out of the driveway, he slung some of the clothes out on the front lawn.

She lowered the window of her Benz and said, "You better not do shit to my clothes."

Shamari took the sleeve of one of her designer dresses and used it to soak the blood that oozed from under his eye. Then, he tossed it in the pile with the rest of the clothing.

With a cigarette lighter in his hand, he said, "I'll burn all this shit up."

She put the car in park and ran out in an attempt to pick up her clothing.

He grabbed her around the waist and she bit into his arm. "Let me go, you bitch-assed nigga!" screamed Jada.

Shamari dropped her on the ground and she bounced up and started swinging wildly at him. "Motherfucker, you're just a goddamned woman beater!"

"Fuck you!"

"No, fuck you and yo broke ass!"

"You fucking no-good ho. How the fuck you gonna call me broke."

"Because you *are* broke, clown."

Across the street, Luke Honeycutt, a 48 year old calculus teacher, sat on his porch eating sunflower seeds when he noticed all the action. Luke wasn't too fond of the young black couple living in the neighborhood. He'd complained to the HOA about the loud music and even said he believed that they were into illegal activities because of the fancy cars. Six months ago he'd secretly called crime stoppers with no valid information. He'd simply told them that he thought his neighbors were up to no good. He yelled to his wife, who was inside the house. "Abigail, will you bring me my cell phone."

She didn't hear. "I need my phone," he called out again.

Luke observed Shamari choking Jada.

Seconds later, a barefoot Abigail passed Luke the phone.

Luke dropped his seeds and galloped across the street, stopping about five feet away from the action and said, "You let her go, or I'm going to call the police. We're not going to tolerate this in this neighborhood."

Shamari lifted Jada off the ground so her feet dangled and then dropped her face-first on to the ground, breaking her new sunglasses into pieces.

He turned to Luke, "Mind you own damn business, cracker!"

Luke said to Abigail, "You go in the house, honey."

Luke didn't know how violent this black thug would get, and he didn't want his wife to witness any violence against him. But Abigail didn't listen to her husband. Instead, she walked across the street yelling, "You're not going to talk to my husband like that, you young punk!"

Luke dialed 911.

Jada attempted to stand up but ended up falling again. She was dizzy and she began to cry before easing over to the pile of clothes. She grabbed a handful and carried them to the car.

Mr. Stanton, the elderly next door neighbor, joined Luke and Abigail. Once they explained to him what was going on, Mr. Stanton asked Jada, "Is everything ok?"

Jada gave him a fake smile and said, "Everything is fine."

Shamari said, "Mind your fucking business, old man."

Jada pulled out of the driveway, and seconds later, Shamari screeched out of the driveway too, going in the opposite direction, but not before Luke snapped a picture of Shamari's license plate with his cell phone.

Shamari arrived at Duke's downtown loft. Duke knew right away something was wrong with his friend but before he had a chance to act, Shamari said, "It went all bad, nigga. All bad."

"You killed her?"

"No, I'm not that crazy, but I beat her ass."

"Bruh, you hit a woman. What the fuck! That shit nowadays is like getting caught with some crack."

Shamari sat on the sofa and Duke sat beside him. "What happened?"

"I don't even know, bruh. I just lost it, man. It's like I was sitting there thinking about how she must have been fucking the dude, giving him head and shit, and I just couldn't take it."

Duke shook his head without saying anything.

"You have to understand. I paid this doctor for the procedures she had and this is the motherfuckin' thanks I get?"

"I know how you feel," Duke said. "Well, no, I don't know how you feel."

"I didn't hit her, but I choked her."

"Same thing, if she calls the police."

"I don't think she would do that, but my nosey-ass neighbors saw the whole thing and I know they called the police." He looked Duke in the eye. "You know the one that's always staring when we pull up?"

"The goofy motherfucker always eating sunflower seeds?"

"Yeah, him."

"He's the one that complained to HOA about the music, right?"

"Well, I don't have no proof it was him, but I'm pretty sure it was his bitch-ass. He saw the whole thing and even came running over in my yard."

"What did you do?"

"I let Jada go and she grabbed her clothes and left."

There was an awkward silence in the room. Finally, Shamari said, "What's up with your cousin?"

"She's called me like 50-11 times since I left you."

"Call her and tell her we will be at South Dekalb Mall in an hour."

Duke called Candace, and she picked up on the first ring.

"Cuzzo, see you in an hour at the spot."

"Cool."

"Remember what I wanted."

"Peyton Manning." Code for eighteen ounces.

"Yeah."

"See you then."

CHAPTER 58

DUKE DROVE HIS DODGE CHARGER AND THEY PULLED UP IN THE MALL parking lot in front of Macy's. He called Candace who told them she was at the food court. "I'm coming inside," said Duke.

Shamari said, "Why are you going in the mall, bruh?"

"They in there eating, man. I mean, what are we going to do, sit out here in the car while they eat?"

Shamari took a deep breath. Duke had a point, but he was anxious to get the work, so he could put it on the street. He needed to make some money. He needed it badly. His mind was still on Jada. He'd hated that he'd put his hands on her. He loved her so much and he couldn't believe that she'd betrayed him for some money. He would have bet anybody that she would be the last person to betray him. Then he thought about all the kilos of cocaine he'd sold, the millions of dollars he'd made and blown, he couldn't help but ask how could he have been so stupid with his money? He was down to less than twenty thousand dollars and needed a way back to the top.

They entered the mall through Macy's and Duke said, "You don't have to meet her if you don't wanna."

Shamari said, "I ain't meeting nobody, bruh. Don't introduce me to nobody."

"You already met Candace before, but you don't 'member. We were teenagers at the time and she wasn't gay then."

"You right, I don't remember and I don't wanna remember. Let's just make this quick, bruh. I got shit to do."

"I feel ya."

When they were inside the food court, Duke spotted Candace and two beautiful women. One was tall and biracial with long hair and the other was short and brown, with an ass that you could play a game of spades on. Candace was a pretty girl herself. A lighter skinned woman with nice skin, she wore a tight fitting black leotard and some running shoes.

Duke and Candace hugged.

Shamari sat at a table in the corner. His mind was still on Jada. He was actually thinking about Louise and how she had vowed to kill him if he put his hands on her daughter. Though he wasn't afraid of Louise, he was ashamed of what he'd done, and he was heartbroken.

Candace signaled for Shamari to come sit with them.

"I'm good."

The brown skinned girl said, "Stay on over there with yo uppity ass."

Duke and all the girls laughed.

Shamari wanted this deal to be over with quick, but he couldn't help but notice how gorgeous Candace's friends were. She was probably licking both of them. Orgies every night. It came with the money. You make lots of money, fuck who you want; when you're broke, you fuck your hand.

Duke came over to the table and said, "Soon as this girl finishes this cheeseburger, we're out."

"Gimme the keys. I'm going to sit in the car."

Duke gave him the keys. Shamari went back out to Duke's car and Duke sat at Candace's table, begging her to let him screw one of the sex kittens, but Candace wasn't having it.

When Shamari made it to the car, he flicked the switch, so he could listen to the radio. R&B music blared through the speakers reminding him of Jada. She loved Chris Brown. He lowered the volume and recounted the money. He didn't want to have any discrepancy about the money. Somebody tapped on the window and he jumped.

"What the fuck?"

Duke laughed, "Scared your punk ass didn't I?"

"That shit ain't funny. You know we in the hood."

Shamari unlocked the door and Duke jumped in on the driver's side.

Shamari said, "So what's up now?"

"They're in front of the mall. Cuzzo said they're in an orange Hummer."

"An orange Hummer! What the fuck? Dude, you've got to be kidding."

"What's wrong?"

"We're about to conduct a fuckin' deal with somebody in a goddamned orange Hummer?"

"Man, this is my cousin. It's all good, homie."

"Ok." Shamari passed him the money.

Duke drove around to the front of the mall. Duke heard somebody honk the horn and to the left of him was the orange Hummer. Duke bounced from the car and got in the backseat of the Hummer."

Rap music came through the speaker.

Shamari got in the driver seat. He wanted to get the hell out of here as fast as he could.

He noticed two niggas with dredlocks in a red Camaro an earshot away. The one closest to him had his head down like he was rolling a blunt.

Candace counted the money. Seconds later, Duke jumped out of the car carrying a Zaire's bag. He came running back to the car, and when he realized Shamari was in the driver seat, he got in on the passenger side.

Shamari sped off and the Hummer drove to the other side of the mall.

Duke said, "It's all good, nigga. I told you Cuzzo was straight."

Shamari pulled out onto Candler road and exited on I-20 when he noticed the two thugs in the red Camaro trailing him. "Bruh, there's a Camaro following us."

Duke glanced over his shoulder. "How you know they following us?"

The Camaro was now damn near banging the rear bumper.

Shamari said, "Look how close they are to us."

"You're right."

"What ya think?"

"Jack Boyz, they must've saw the deal go down at the mall."

Shamari said, "Ya think? Bright ass orange Hummer."

Duke said, "Step on it, homie."

Shamari sped up but the Camaro was right on their ass.

Duke unbuckled his seat belt and grabbed a 9mm that was stuffed between the two seats.

"I'm 'bout to bus at these clowns."

Duke eased the window down and positioned himself to where he was hanging out of the window. He aimed his gun at the window of the Camaro and fired two shots. One bullet shattered the glass on the passenger side of the Camaro.

A blue siren flashed on the dashboard.

Shamari said, "Ah shit! Cops!"

Duke sat back in the car. "Don't stop driving."

Shamari pressed the gas to the floor. Duke removed a pocket knife from his pocket and ripped into the package of coke and threw the coke out of the window. It looked like a trail of flour blowing in the wind.

Three Georgia State Patrol cars were now visible, and they all had their sirens on.

Shamari said, "Bruh, I'm going to stop at the next exit."

"Man, punch this motherfucker! You driving like my nana. I can't go back to jail, homie. I'm getting life if we get caught."

"I'm doing ninety."

"Well, do a hundred."

"And kill us both?"

"I'm dead if we get caught."

The highway curved and Shamari slowed down.

"Don't stop, bruh. I'm telling you, don't stop this motherfucker."

"I ain't stopping. I had to slow down for the curve."

Now there were six law enforcement cars behind him.

Duke continued to pour coke out the window. "Don't you stop this goddamned car until this coke is gone. I don't wanna go to jail for the rest of my life."

One of the state patrolmen spoke through a bullhorn. "Pull over or else we're shooting."

At 90 mph, Shamari attempted to speed up while still maintaining control.

The state troopers fired a shot at the tire but missed.

The cop on the passenger side of the Camaro fired a shot and blasted the right rear tire of the charger. Duke's car fishtailed before flipping over the median. The car was now lying upside down in the middle of the median.

Duke opened the door of the upside down car, jumped out the car, and fled with his gun in his hand.

One of the patrolmen shouted, "Stop or I'm going to shoot." And when the patrolman saw the gun in Duke's hand, he fired two shots. The bullets ripped into Duke's back. Duke dropped to his knees and seconds later, crumbled to the ground where Duke took his last breath.

Shamari's door was jammed. He kicked it, but it would not give in. There was no running for him. He surrendered. "Fuck" was all he kept saying over and over as they dragged him out of the car and cuffed him before they sat him down in the grass near the road. Onlookers drove by slowly trying to see what was going on.

One person said, "You goddamned criminal! Wasting taxpayer dollars!"

Another one said. "It's gonna be okay."

A third person yelled. "Fuck the police!"

Shamari wanted it to all be over. He hoped it was a bad dream. He glanced over at Duke and saw the paramedics taking his pulse. One of them said, "He's dead."

Shamari saw the white's of Duke's eyes. He didn't know what made him feel worse—the fact that his friend was dead or the fact he was going to jail, perhaps to prison, for a very long time.

CHAPTER 59

SHAMARI'S MOTHER CALLED JADA AND TOLD HER THAT HE'D BEEN locked up. At first, Jada thought it was because of the domestic violence. She was sure Luke and Abigail had told the police everything they knew about the fight. But Shamari's mother assured her it was new drug charges. She told Jada there was no bond set but she could go visit him on Thursday. When Jada checked the Fulton county jail, she saw his mug shot and the charges were listed underneath—attempted possession of cocaine.

Jada was pissed with Shamari for hitting her, but there was no way she was going to let him go through this alone. He'd been there for her, so she would at least visit him on Thursday.

Jada sat on the other side of the glass window waiting on Shamari. She wore another pair of Jackie-O sunglasses—a brown version. She knew it would be emotional seeing him behind bars. Though she'd been unfaithful, she still loved that man.

When Shamari came out, the first thing she noticed was that the orange jumpsuit was too small and the second thing she noticed was the cut under his eye and the bandages on his elbow. He sat down and picked up the phone. He was hesitant to say anything. He didn't know what to say.

She said, "Hey!"

"Hey, babe."

"What happened to your eye? Did they do something to you?"

"Who?"

"The police. Did they hurt your eye?"

He laughed and said, "No, you did this remember?"

She'd forgotten all about the fight at that moment. All she could think about was he was in jail. Then she said, "I went by the house. Looks like the police paid us a visit. The place had been ransacked and they took your Bentley, along with one of my jewelry boxes."

"How do you know it was them and not some robbers?"

"Nosey-ass Luke told me. Seemed like he was happy. I can't stand his bitch ass."

He laughed. He held his arm up and let her get a closer look at the bandages. "This happened during the wreck"

"Wreck?"

"Mama didn't tell you 'bout the wreck?"

"No, she just told me you'd been arrested."

"Man, you ain't gone believe what happened?"

"Don't say nothing. You know how these phones are."

Shamari said, "I know there is so much I wanna tell you. You member G don't you?"

"G?" Jada looked confused.

"Yeah, dude from my hood that works here."

G was short for Gerald. He'd grown up with Shamari and Duke. Now, he was a jailer

"I remember him vaguely."

"He's gonna give you a kite."

"Ok. Cool."

"Duke is dead?"

"What do you mean he's dead?"

"Man, we led the police on a high speed chase. You must not have been paying attention to the news."

"It happened on I-20?"

"Yeah."

"Yeah, my friend Skyy told me about it. Said the car turned over."

Shamari cut his eye at the overweight jailer glancing at his watch. He knew time was running out, and there was so much he wanted to tell her, but it would have to wait. He would have to explain it all in a letter.

"What can I do to help you?"

"I need an attorney. A big time attorney. With my record, I'm fucked if I can't get a lawyer."

"There is no more money, right?"

"None."

Shamari dropped his head again. He never knew it would end like this.

Jada put her hand up to the glass and smiled. "Bae', I got you. I'm gonna do whatever I gotta do to pay for a lawyer."

His hand touched the glass.

"I'm so sorry that I hurt you. I'll always love you," said Jada

Shamari was about to say he loved her when the fat jailer said, "Times up. Let's go, big boy."

Shamari stood and headed back to the jungle. He glanced back at Jada who was still standing there in a fitted dress which hugged her ass and her cleavage causing both to be very pronounced. They made eye contact for the last time. Goddamned, she looked good.

CHAPTER 60

BLACK, LANI AND KYRIE WERE AT LANI'S MOTHER'S HOUSE.
"I swear to God on everything I love Im'ma kill that bitch-assed nigga," Black said. He limped on one crutch because one of the bullets had fractured his fibula.

"Shhh," Lani said trying to keep him quiet.

"Tyrann, quit all that cursing out now. You're going to respect my house," Lani's mother yelled from the next room."

Lani said, "I told you mama can hear everything. Matter of fact, I believe she's in there listening to us."

Black said, "My bad, Ms. Carolyn, I forgot you were in there."

"It's okay. Just don't do it again and if you do, don't talk so loud. You know how your voice carries."

Kyrie said, "I always told you, you were a loud motherfucker."

Black said, "You shut the fuck up." But he'd lowered his voice this time so Ms. Carolyn couldn't hear him.

Lani said, "I don't want you to get in any trouble."

Black said, "I can't believe you're safeguarding this clown. This nigga cheats on you and then tell you to get the fuck out of his house. Who does that?"

Lani said, "You weren't no angel."

"Okay, I had some babies outside the relationship, but I always took care of you."

"Money doesn't solve everything," said Lani.

Black said, "Show me something it doesn't solve."

"Money can't hold you at night."

Black said, "But you damn sure can hold money at night."

Kyrie giggled.

Lani said, "You missing the point. When I was with you, I had everything I wanted, but I wanted you to be at home with me sometimes."

Black said, "I know and I know what's important. One thing I thought about when I was lying up in that hospital bed was I'd made a lot of money and I'd fucked the finest bitches, but I really didn't have nobody that I could call wifey. You're the closest thing to my wifey and you're with another man. But you know that God spared Black for a reason, and I'm going to make the best of my life."

"I like hearing you talk like that."

"I like talking."

The doorbell rang and when Lani opened it, Jada was standing there. She looked sad.

Black saw Jada and said, "Hey, baby girl, long time."

Jada smiled and said, "Glad that you're still with us."

Black limped across the other side of the room and hugged her. "I'm bulletproof."

Jada said, "Okay, Superman."

Black said, "Seriously, it's good to see you."

Lani could just tell from Jada's energy that something wasn't right. "What's wrong, chica?"

"Man, it's Shamari."

"Did he put his hands on you?"

Jada didn't want to tell her about the fight right now. She would discuss that later.

"Did that nigga hit you?"

Black and Kyrie looked on, waiting for her to answer the question. Black knew Shamari. They had done state time together, and they used to gamble, but they'd never done any business together.

Jada said, "No."

"What's wrong with him?"

"He's locked up?"

"For what?"

"I don't even know. All I know is there was a high-speed chase on I-20."

Black sat down and rested the crutch over his lap. "Wait a minute. I saw that shit on the news. Those niggas were driving and dumping coke out the window, right?"

Jada said, "I don't know the details."

Black said, "Yeah, I saw that shit on the news yesterday. It's like they were in a movie or something. I saw that shit live on Eye in the Sky."

"Well, I guess that was them," Jada said.

Black said, "Damn, I feel bad for Shamari. His record just as bad as mine. He's fucked. He's gonna need a miracle."

Jada turned to Black, "You know a good lawyer?"

"How much you trying to spend?" Black said.

Jada said, "That's the other thing, there is no money."

Black said, "No good lawyer is going to work for free."

Jada said, "Oh, you can believe Im'ma come up with the money if I have to sell every goddamned thing in my closet."

Black said, "Damn, you ride or die, li'l mama."

Jada said, "I gotta be that way for somebody that has done so much for me and my family."

Black turned to Kyrie, "Where's the book bag?"

Kyrie passed him a backpack that had been resting on the floor.

Black dug into the backpack and removed three stacks of cash and tossed two stacks to Lani. "That's ten grand, get you an apartment." Then he tossed Jada 5 stacks. "Here this is to help you with Shamari's legal fee."

Jada tried to hand it back.

Black grinned and said, "Hell, I probably owe him this anyway. I've cheated on his yella ass so many times at the poker table."

Everybody laughed.

Black smiled at Lani and said, "I told you I was gonna get you back, didn't I?"

"Black, we ain't back together."

"That's what you think," Black said.

Gunshots rang out and bullets crashed through Ms Carolyn's window. Everybody hit the floor.

Jada said, "What the fuck?"

Ms Carolyn screamed from the other room, "What the hell is going on?"

Lani made her way over to the window and peeked over the window sill and pulled the curtain back. Nothing but darkness.

When everybody was back on their feet, Ms Carolyn came into the room with her cell phone in hand.

Black looked at the sixteen shots that had been fired into the wall and said, "I bet your boy, Chris, had something to do with this."

"Who, Chris? Hell, no! He wouldn't do nothing like this."

Jada said, "When I was walking up, I saw two dudes in an old black pathfinder creep by looking like they were lost."

"See! Jada knows Chris. If it was him, she would have said so," Lani said.

Jada said, "I couldn't tell you who it was."

Black said, "I swear to God, Im'ma kill that motherfucker."

Lani said, "My mama told you to stop cussin' a few minutes ago."

Ms Carolyn said, "If he's responsible for this, Tyrann, Im'ma help you kill his bitch ass." Then she called the police.

CHAPTER 61

TREY DROVE TO MONTE'S MOTHER'S HOUSE. MONTE CAME OUT ON
the porch barefoot, smoking a Newport. He's lost so much weight since
the last time Trey had seen him that he asked him if he was smoking
crack.

"Hell, no! Why you say that?"

"Bruh, you looking bad."

"Shit, you would be looking bad too if you were looking at ten." He blew
out a smoke ring and said, "It's called stress, my brother. You would
know nothing 'bout that. You got money. You got bitches. And more than
that, you'll be on the streets for the next ten years."

"Ten years."

"Ten years, or tell where I was going with the drugs and where I get
them from. They know I'm a mule."

"How do they know that?"

"What big time drug dealer you know live with their mama?"

Trey said, "Actually, you're the only person I know over thirty that lives
at home."

"Exactly!"

Trey laughed and Monte said, "What's so funny?"

"What so funny?" The other night at Kroger's?" said Trey

"What about it?"

"I thought you were trying to set me up."

"Naw, bruh." Monte dropped the cigarette butt and kicked some sand on it with his bare feet before lighting another.

"I'm dead serious."

Monte puffed his Newport and said, "Get the fuck outta here, bruh." He laughed, but then he was disappointed. "Really? You thought I was gonna set you up."

"I put that on everything."

"Look, I did some stupid shit to put myself in this position. There is no way I'm gonna take you under with me, homie. You've done so much for me."

" 'Preciate it."

"No, I appreciate you."

Trey said, "So, what about the girl?"

"What about her?"

"Do we have to worry about her talking?"

"No, I'm pleading guilty under the condition that they let her go."

Trey said, "Good deal."

"So are you going to do what you're supposed to do? For me taking the fall."

Trey looked confused trying to figure out what in the hell Monte was talking about.

"I'm broke as hell, homie. You took care of the legal fees, but I need some money. I need to give my mama some money. Need to make sure she is alright while I'm gone."

"What kind of money you talking about?"

"Just money so she can get a new car to drive to see me. And if you can give her some bread every month to help out with her bills."

"Dude, I'm going to take care of you."

Monte believed him. He knew Trey was a man of his word. That was the only reason he never considered ratting. If it had been anybody else, he would have considered it. A lot.

CHAPTER 62

JADA WAS UPSTAIRS AT CRAIG'S TOWNHOUSE WHEN SHE HEARD THE door open. She hated the fact that he would just show up anytime he felt like it without calling, but today she wasn't mad. She was actually happy he'd shown up. When he came upstairs, she kissed him and said, "Baby, help me carry my clothes to my car."

He looked confused, "Why are you carrying the clothes to the car? You're supposed to be moving in, not moving out."

She said, "I got something to tell you. Promise not to be upset with me."

He took a deep breath. "What is it, Jada?"

She grabbed his hand and he pulled away and she grabbed his hand again. This time she pulled him close to her, and wrapped her arms around him. She kissed his lips.

"What is it?"

She kissed him again.

He said, "I promise. I'm not going to get mad."

"Look, I'm moving in with my mother."

"In the ghetto?"

"Well, I guess so."

"That wretched-ass place?"

She laughed because she thought it was so cute when he tried to talk slang. "Babe, the word is 'ratchet' , not wretched."

"Whatever. Look, let me get this straight. You'd rather be in the ghetto hearing gunshots and shit than live in a gated townhouse?"

"Well, it's not that I would rather be. It's just that I'm a grown woman and I don't wanna be here and have nothing to call my own.

"What's mine is yours."

"This townhouse is not in my name. That Maserati is not in my name. It's not even the color I would have picked."

She knew she sounded like a spoiled brat, but that was her goddamned intention. She was trying to prove a point.

"But you're going back to the hood?"

"Yeah."

"So what made you decide that?"

"I was just thinking."

Craig laughed and said, "You're fucking crazy." Then, he grabbed a handful of her clothes and started walking toward the stairs. He wasn't supposed to help her move out. She'd counted on him begging and doing whatever it took for her to stay at his place. She caught up to him before he reached the stairs and put her arms around him. "Baby I don't want you to think I'm ungrateful. I'm so grateful for all that you do."

"But you're moving back to the hood."

He turned and faced her. She dropped to her knees and unzipped his pants and took him deep inside her mouth. She could feel his dick in the back her throat. She licked the shaft and sucked his balls. She massaged his prostate until he exploded in her mouth. She swallowed all his seed and then she kissed him. This is one thing she liked about him. Even when she swallowed his cum, he would kiss her. That was one thing Shamari would never do.

Between kisses he asked, "What do you want me to do?"

"I want you to make me happy as you see fit."

"What do you need? Money?"

"I need to be comfortable. I need access to cash if I'm going to give up living with Shamari for this. Gimme seven thousand dollars a month, and put the Maserati in my name."

"Oh no, I'm not doing that."

"Well it's not really mine then. Stop saying it's mine then."

He took a deep breath and said, "I'll put the one that I own in your name. Since it's the older.

She beamed. "Really, you would do that for me?"

"I told you I would take care of you."

She kissed him and kneeled again and took him in her mouth again. She intended to suck him dry. Literally.

CHAPTER 63

SHAMARI'S CHILDHOOD FRIEND GERALD, THE JAILER, CALLED JADA and said to meet him at the food court in Lennox Mall in thirty minutes. She was running fifteen minutes behind when she approached the man that fit the description that he'd given her over the phone. Gerald was 6'4, brown skinned, and slender with a bald head and no facial hair. She could tell he was hood, but he wasn't about to break the law. He loved his jailer job. Gerald and Shamari had known each other since they were eight years old and even played on the same pee-wee football team.

"Gerald."

"Yeah," he grinned and said, "Goddamn, them boys at the county jail was right."

Jada looked confused.

"Man, after you left the jail, everybody in the jail was talking about how goddamn fine you were."

Jada grinned. Not really knowing what to make of Gerald's compliment. Hell, the men in jail just wanted to see a woman. Any woman. They were all horny as hell.

Gerald, staring with a silly ass look on his face, finally said, "I know I couldn't afford a woman like you."

Jada smiled not wanting to be arrogant and not really wanting to tell broke-ass Gerald there was no way in hell she would go out with a jailer.

Gerald said, "Do you want something to drink? A soda, a hot dog or something?"

She wouldn't dare eat that disgusting-ass food court trash. But again she had to be nice. "No thanks."

Gerald pulled out an old-ass flip phone and said, "Can I take a picture of you?"

Jada said, "Why not." But he was getting to be annoying with all this admiration. If his phone wasn't so damn old, there was no way she'd let him take a picture of her. But since he had a flip phone, she knew he couldn't post on Facebook or Instagram. Even if he did, she was sure with his two megapixels, it would be blurry as hell.

Jada said, "Gerald, I really am flattered by all the admiration, but can you get to the point? Don't you have something for me?"

"Oh yeah." He dug into his pocket and removed a folded piece of notebook paper and passed it to her.

On the paper, Shamari had written,

Man, first let me begin by saying how much I appreciate what you're doing for me. Man, how do I begin? First, let me say that I don't know where to begin. Duke is dead. Like I told you earlier. He got gunned down by one of the officers.

But I guess you can say I got desperate and I trusted him to have a connection, Candace, his cousin. She's a dyke bitch that turned out to be an informant. We were supposed to get a half a brick from her. She kept trying to front us more, which should've clued me in that something wasn't right, but I guess since it was his cousin, I trusted her. Somebody I didn't know or even talked to about drugs and here I am in a goddamned jam. I'm sure Duke didn't know it though. I say that because he was pouring the coke out the window when he found out it was the police. Which makes the shit even more scandalous. This bitch tried to set her own cousin up. But you know how it is out here now, every man for himself. You're probably wondering why didn't I fuck with Trey? Well I tried, but he didn't want to work with me when he found out about the little situation with Tony. But anyway there is an attorney named Joey Turch, he's young but he's a beast and he's expensive. Hire him if you can. He can get me out of this, if anybody can. If not he can make it tolerable.

Jada stood from the table and noticed that the clown, Gerald, was still staring at her. She said, "Thanks, Gerald."

Gerald frowned and said, "Shamari said you would have something for me."

"What?"

"Well he just said you would look out for me. You know a hundred, two hundred dollars, whatever you can spare."

Jada dug into her pocket and passed him a hundred dollar bill.

Gerald grinned and said, "Can we take one picture together."

Jada said, "I ain't gonna be sitting here taking pictures with you all day and pay you."

Gerald said, "It's all good. I appreciate it and if you need me for anything, you got my number."

Jada thought what in the hell would she possibly need Gerald for. When she got on the escalator, she knew his perverted ass was watching her, so she switched a little as she skipped to the escalator knowing he was dreaming about pussy he would never get.

CHAPTER 64

JOEY TURCH WAS AN ARROGANT LITTLE SON-OF-A-BITCH. JADA KNEW that by the personalized license plate that he had on his Porsche Panamera. The tag read *SetUfree*. Joey was thirty-four years old, with dark black hair and a funny looking nose. Jada thought he might have been Jewish, but she wasn't sure. He wore a designer suit and expensive shoes. Jada sat across from his desk. She had dressed conservative today by her standards, but she still wore a pencil skirt that made her ass look fantastic and she showed just a hint of cleavage. Her objective was not to turn Joey on, but hell, she was still very much a woman and a sexy one at that. She would use what she had to get what she wanted if the opportunity presented itself.

Joey said, "So let me get this straight. Shamari never talked to the informant on the phone."

"No. Not about drugs."

"But he spoke to her?"

"I think so."

"What was the conversation about?"

"I don't know."

Joey looked intent like something wasn't sounding right. His facial expression seemed as if he didn't believe Jada.

Jada said, "Maybe you can go visit Shamari down at the jail. He can tell you more."

Joey said, "Good idea, but you're going to have to hire me first."

"That's what I'm here for."

Joey's eye's zeroed in on the cleavage for a split second, long enough for him to decide they were implants. Then he glanced at the designer bag and diamond bracelet. There was some money somewhere.

Jada asked, "When can you go?"

"Go where?"

"To see Shamari."

"After I'm retained."

"What are your fees?"

"I'm very expensive, but I can make this little case go away or get him a good plea."

"I heard that a good lawyer never makes promises."

"That's true...well unless your name is Joey Turch."

"What makes you so special?"

"Well let me see...I'm connected, smart and a good trial lawyer."

All these things Joey said were true, but what really helped him was one particular case where he defended a kingpin that was facing multiple life sentences. Joey beat all the drug charges and the kingpin was convicted for money laundering. He received eight years for money laundering, and ever since then, Joey became the go-to-guy for the Atlanta Dope boys.

Joeys face became serious. "I need to see Shamari, and after he tells me what happened, I'll go to the D.A. to get the discovery and see what they have on him. Then we'll decide if we're going to trial or not. Or if I can get him a good plea"

"How much are your fees?"

"Twenty thousand. If I have to go to trial, it will be twice that."

"For a state case? This is not a fed case."

Joey smiled and said, "And I am not cheap. I mean you can always take your chances with another attorney."

"I don't have twenty thousand dollars."

Joey sat in silence. He'd seen it time and time again—young, black drug dealer's girlfriends come through his office with ten thousand dollars worth of clothing on but not enough money to pay him.

"How much do you have?"

"I've got about ten thousand dollars."

"And you're driving a Maserati."

"How did you know that?"

"I saw you pull up."

"And?"

"You can sign that car over to me until you come up with the money."

"Fuck no!"

"Well, you're going to have to come up with the money."

Jada sat there thinking about how she would come up with the money. She'd actually considered selling the Maserati, but it wasn't in her name yet.

"How soon do you need the money?"

"I'll go see Shamari tomorrow. I'll need the money by the end of the week."

Jada stood and shook Joey's hand. As she walked out of his office, Joey's eyes were on her ass. He thought her ass looked like two volleyballs under that skirt.

CHAPTER 65

JADA WAS WEARING A WHITE G-STRING AND SIX INCH HEELS. HER breasts sitting prominent and her body was oiled. She was looking delicious.

Craig sat on the edge of the bed when Jada came out of the bathroom. His eyes went from her boobs, to her heels, and then to her tiny-ass waistline. He imagined himself gripping it as he pounded her pussy from behind. His dick was so hard he could scream.

Seconds later, she was on her knees stroking him as he looked on with anticipation, wishing she would hurry up and put it in her mouth.

She kissed his dick and stood.

"Where are you going?"

"I got a surprise for you."

He smiled. "What? What? What?"

"Quit acting like a baby, goddamn it."

She disappeared into the bathroom and a minute later she backed out. He was still sitting on the edge of the bed.

"Where is the surprise?" His dick had now shriveled

"Close your eyes."

He closed him eyes, expecting her to give him head with ice in her mouth or pop rocks. She'd done this before. The pop rocks made a bunch of noise and he really didn't like it but the ice had made him scream.

"Okay, you can open your eyes."

When Craig opened his eyes, Jada's friend, Skyy, burst through the bathroom door. She was wearing a white teddy and heels that elevated her ass to perfection. Skyy's body was all natural and though he was a surgeon, he could appreciate an amazing natural body.

He grinned and said, "What the hell?"

Skyy said, "Shhh."

Craig fell backward on the bed and Jada sat on his face. He sucked and gnawed on her clit like it was a peach.

Skyy sucked and licked Craig's balls until his dick rose and she placed a condom on him with her mouth. Though Jada trusted Craig, Skyy didn't know him that well. After the condom was secure, she jumped on his dick and rode him until he was about to cum.

He pushed her off him.

"What the fuck is wrong with this white boy?" Skyy said.

"Nothing wrong with me. I was about to ejaculate."

"Ejaculate? Why the fuck are you so technical? I feel like I'm in a sex ed class."

"Well I was about to cum."

Jada said, "Well that's what you're supposed to do."

"Not yet."

Skyy eased over to Jada and gripped Jada's left ass cheek. Jada turned to her and they kissed.

Jada fell on the bed beside Craig, and Skyy began performing oral sex on Jada.

Craig, now with the condom off, was stroking his dick and enjoying the performance of the women.

Jada moaned and she grabbed the back of Skyy's head and face fucked her. It felt good. Better than Craig or Shamari or any other man who had gone down on her. But she kept telling herself she didn't like girls.

Jada's body trembled as her knees jerked. She came so vigorously, she yelled. "Shit! Goddamn! Whooo!"

Craig had never seen her cum like that. He never made her say all these things. For a split second, he wondered if he had ever turned her on.

Jada and Skyy began kissing, while Craig was still stroking his dick.

Skyy pulled Craig into the circle. She pulled away from Jada and kissed him

His hand was now on Skyy's ass. He shoved his fingers inside her V-J. It was so wet. When he removed his finger, he sucked her juices off.

Skyy pushed his head between her legs and said. "If you really wanna taste this pussy, white boy, taste it." Then she looked at Jada. "Since this selfish bitch don't like to eat pussy."

Jada laughed and said, "Never in a million years."

While Craig was gnawing away at Skyy's love box, Jada sucked his balls from behind. The threesome enjoyed themselves until everybody came and passed out.

The next morning, after Skyy had gone, Craig and Jada chatted while eating Kashi GoLean crunch and sitting at the breakfast table.

Jada said, "I can't believe you didn't go home last night."

"Why?"

"Um, you're married remember?"

He dug into his cereal bowl and said, "I'm away at a conference in California."

"What the fuck? You're a good liar."

"I'm not lying. There really was a conference last night. Me, you and Diamond."

"Whose Diamond?"

"You're friend."

Jada laughed, "You mean Skyy."

"I don't know why I wanna keep calling her Diamond."

Jada ate her cereal. "I guess since they're both stripper nicknames."

"Maybe."

Jada sipped from the water glass in front of her and then said, "I need your help with something."

"What?"

"Well it's Skyy."

"What about her?"

"She's about to get evicted. I need you to help me pay her rent."

"How much is her rent?"

"Well, she's three months behind."

 Craig dropped his spoon in the cereal bowl handle first. Then he dug it out and licked the almond milk from his hand. "

"Help her with her rent. She's three months behind."

She made a sad face and he asked how much?

"I need five thousand dollars." The five thousand dollars would give her exactly what she needed to pay the attorney.

"Five thousand dollars is a lot of money."

"I know and I'm sorry that I have to ask you for it, but she is a friend" She made another sad face.

"Is this what this was all about? Me helping your friend. Is this why you surprised me?"

"Hell, no! I remembered once you said you'd never had a ménage"

"If I would have known it was going to cost me, I wouldn't have participated."

"You said you would give me what I wanted. I guess that was all lies, just to get me to stay at your cheap-ass townhouse."

The townhouse was quite expensive, but Jada said that to bruise his fragile little ego.

"There is nothing cheap about this townhouse. You sound ungrateful."

"No. I don't mean to sound ungrateful, but she's my friend."

Craig and Jada made eye contact for a long time, but there was an awkward silence between them. Finally she said, "Will you sign the goddamned car title over to me then?"

"I said I would, so I am."

CHAPTER 66

AFTER RECEIVING INFORMATION FROM A STRIPPER NAMED ISIS, BLACK found Chris's whereabouts and had his goons tail him. Chris was on his cell phone at the Cactus Car Wash when an ex-con named K.B. approached him and slapped the fuck out him. When Chris threw up his hands to try and fight K.B., two more goons hopped out of an Expedition. One of them began smashing security cameras with a baseball bat.

A couple of female customers screamed when they saw all the ruckus going on.

A balding middle age manager approached the fight and K.B. slapped the fuck out of him too. K.B. hit the manager so hard that he left a palm-print on the side of the manager's face.

The goons then threw Chris into the back of a moving Cadillac Escalade. K.B. and the goons followed the Escalade in their Expedition.

In the Cadillac, Chris was blindfolded and everyone drove to a subdivision in Riverdale. K.B. and another goon brought Chris inside a house and set him on a sofa and removed the blindfold. With an AR-15 pointed at Chris's dome, a short, stocky dude named Twan dared Chris to move. "I'm just itching to make soup out of yo brain, motherfucker."

Chris said, "So what you want? Money? If you want money, you're going to have to let me go get it or call my brother."

Twan said, "Motherfucker, don't say shit until I ask you to say something."

Seconds later Black stepped into the room on crutches and smiled at Chris. He then sat beside him and offered his hand. Chris declined.

Chris heart was about to burst though his chest. It was beating so hard Black could hear it.

Black said, "You're probably thinking I'm gonna kill you, don't you?"

No answer.

"K.B., show this nigga we not playing with him."

K.B. fired a shot into Chris's foot. Chris hollered then said, "Just do what the fuck you're going to do to me."

Twan said, "Didn't I tell you not to say a motherfuckin' thing." The A.R.-15 was directly at his temple now.

"What do you want from me?"

Twan slapped him with the gun and Black said, "Chill out, Twan." Then he turned to Chris. "Okay, where is the motherfuckin' money."

"I ain't got no money."

"A dope boy without money. Who do you think I am? You think I believe that shit?"

"Bruh, just go ahead and kill me."

"What if I don't wanna kill you?"

"There is no money." Chris said, thinking about the stash that his brother had, but the last thing he needed to do was subject his brother to this.

Black leaned into Chris until their noses were almost touching. "You should have finished me, clown," Black whispered.

"What're you talking about?"

Twan and K.B. hogtied Chris.

Black said, "So where is the work?"

"What you talking about?"

Black said, "That's a nice looking Benz your mother driving."

Chris said, "What?"

"That is your mama with the Black 550?"

K.B. said, "We started to run up in her crib and lay everybody down."

Black said, "I don't believe in hurting women and kids. Unless."

"Unless what?" Chris said.

"I don't get what I want."

It was obvious to Chris that Black knew who his mother was. He didn't want anything to happen to her.

"That's a nice-ass house she got in Decatur too?"

Chris said, "Look, bruh, I got work at this house in Sandy Springs. But you leave my mama out of this."

Black said, "If there's a stash there that's worth something, I swear to God, you're mama's safe."

Chris said, "Listen, man, I'll show you exactly how to get there."

CHAPTER 67

JOEY TURCH CALLED JADA AND SAID HE HAD SOME GOOD NEWS AND suggested that they met in his office right away. Jada was there fifteen minutes later.

Joey looked at Jada and said, "I spoke with Shamari and I spoke with the D.A. They have a pretty weak case."

Jada smiled. "Oh really?"

"Yes. Seems like Markel Ferguson's cousin was working as an informant."

"Markel who? I know this some bullshit. Shamari don't know no Markel"

Joey looked at her like she was dumb as hell and said, "I'm talking about the deceased guy."

"Duke?"

"Yes, Markel is his real name."

"I never knew that."

Joey continued. "She set them up, but Shamari never spoke about drugs with her on the phone. He never talked about drugs, so they can't charge him with attempted possession. Shamari can only be charged as an accomplice."

"An accomplice to a drug crime? I didn't know there was such a crime."

"Well, they're going to charge him with conspiracy, but it's state conspiracy so it will be easy to beat."

"You can beat this?"

"Ferguson is dead and Shamari never talked to the cousin. So they have a weak case."

"So, why haven't he got a bond?"

"His record is pretty bad."

"So he's gonna go free."

Joey smiled. "I can promise you this. If he doesn't go free, he's not doing over a year in prison. The only thing that's keeping me from promising complete freedom is his jail record."

Jada took a deep breath. She was glad Shamari wouldn't be going away for a long time though she knew her relationship with him was basically over. He didn't deserve a long prison sentence.

Joey said, "So what about my money?"

"I don't have it all?"

"How much do you have?"

"I have about ten thousand."

He smiled and said, "So you know what this means?"

"What?"

"The Maserati."

"I'll have to bring it back tomorrow."

"Along with the title?"

"It's not in my name, yet."

"Why?"

"Well, it's been signed over to me, but the title hasn't come back in my name."

"It's registered to you, right?"

"Yeah."

"Well, I'm going to draw up some paperwork. You're agreeing that you're going to give me possession of the car when you get the title and I'm going to need a copy of the key

"The key for what?"

He grinned, "It will be easier to take possession, if for some reason you don't want to give it up."

"Okay," Jada said removing a key ring and handing it over to Joey. "Sheesh. You're one thirsty-ass lawyer."

"But I'm the best, and when you're the best at something, you should get paid like the best."

CHAPTER 68

IT WAS 1:00 AM AND TREY'S PHONE KEPT RINGING. HE THOUGHT HE heard it, but he was half asleep until Starr said, "Who in the fuck is calling you this late at night?"

Trey rolled over groggily and said, "What, babe?"

"What babe, my ass. Who is calling you, Trey?"

Trey sat up in the bed and grabbed his cell phone from the dresser. It was Monte. He showed Starr the phone to calm her down. Just a couple of days ago, Lani had told her the story of how Chris used a dude's name in his directory in the place of a bitch he was fucking. Starr wasn't having it. She stood from the bed and said, "Trey, call Monte back."

Trey dialed Monte's number.

"Put him on speaker-phone!"

"Goddamn."

Starr said, "I know how ya'll niggas operate."

Monte said, "Trey, I need to talk to you right away."

"What's wrong?"

"I don't wanna speak over the phone."

"Where do you wanna meet?"

"You name the place."

"IHOP on Ponce de Leon.

Starr said, "I'm going."

"Okay, meet me at Magic City in an hour," said Trey.

"Bet."

An hour later, Starr and Trey entered IHOP on Ponce de Leon. Monte was sitting alone in a booth in the back of the restaurant.

Monte spotted Starr first and thought even in sweatpants with no makeup on, she was one bad bitch. He wished he was Trey for just one night.

Trey approached the table and shook Monte's hand. Then he and Starr sat in the booth. Starr was in the inside, of course.

The waitress came and Trey and Monte both ordered coffee and Starr ordered pancakes. She wasn't hungry but she wanted pancakes since they were at IHOP.

Monte was still looking at Starr but was hesitant to talk because he'd never known Trey to discuss business around his girl.

Trey said, "It's okay, bruh. You can talk around her. It's all good."

"It's ugly, bruh, real ugly."

"What's ugly?" Talk to me."

Monte avoided Trey's eyes and said, "She's talking. The girl is talking."

Trey said, "What the fuck you mean she's talking? Talking on who?"

"You."

"This bitch don't even know me. How is she talking about me?"

Monte sipped his water as Starr looked at him with suspicion, trying to analyze Monte. Trying to see if he was a believable person or not.

Monte said, "You're right, she don't know you."

"So, how is she talking about me?"

There was a long silence.

The waitress dropped Starr's pancakes on the table and asked, "Do you need anything else?"

Starr said, "I'm fine."

Soon as the waitress left, Trey said, "Talk to me, bruh."

Monte looked at Starr's pancakes, not because he was hungry but because he didn't want to face Trey. Finally, he said, "Look, I know I told you I only took her down with me but one time. That was a lie."

"What?"

"Yeah, I took her with me at least ten times. So she knew the whole operation."

Trey said, "She knows who my connect is?"

"No. I never took her nowhere near the connect."

"What the fuck does she know?"

"She came with me to your house one night. She was in the car, ducking down."

"She knows who I am?"

"No, but she does know your name is Trey"

"How do you know she's talking?"

Starr took one bite from her pancakes, but she didn't feel like eating. She didn't want the damn pancakes. The fact that Trey might be in trouble terrified her. Not because he couldn't handle it, but because she didn't want her man to go to prison. What would she do?

"I flew to Texas yesterday to sign my plea agreement."

"Yeah, I knew that. Ten years right?"

"Well, actually, I got sixty-three months."

Trey looked at him suspiciously. Wondering how in the hell he got so little time.

"I know you're thinking how did I get it? Well actually, my attorney said I'm getting sentenced at the right time. They just did away with mandatory minimum sentences and they knew I was just a mule."

There was a long silence. "You can call any lawyer in Atlanta. They will tell you what I'm telling you is true."

Starr believed him and so did Trey.

"Okay, you signed your plea."

"Yes."

"And what happened?"

"When I was about to leave, my lawyer said the DEA wanted to talk to me. Said I could talk to them if I wanted to, but I didn't have to talk."

"And you did what?"

"I wanted to hear what they had to say, and I'm glad I did."

"And what did they ask you?"

"They wanted to know who Trey Carter is."

"And you said?"

"I don't know him. And they said I was lying and I said I'm not. Then they showed me a picture of me and you at Lennox Mall."

"What the fuck? How did the Houston DEA get a pic of you and me?"

"Well, I'm sure somebody in Atlanta took the pic. This is Feds, bruh."

Starr said, "Maybe they were following you."

Monte said, "You didn't tell me you went to jail."

"Huh?"

"They said that you just got out of jail."

Trey said, "My neighbors told you I went to jail."

Monte said, "Oh yeah, they did. I forgot. But the DEA knows that you just got out of jail too."

Trey thought maybe Monte was lying. But why would he lie?

Monte said, "It's the girl. The feds asked me why would I want to go away and let you live in your nice big house. And do time for you."

"My big house?"

"What I'm telling you, bruh, is that the girl told them about how nice your house is."

Trey was silent for a long time, finally he said, "I gotta find this bitch and deal with her."

Trey stood and dropped a twenty dollar bill on the table for the waitress. Starr and Monte followed Trey to the parking lot.

Trey was parked next to Monte's mother's car

Monte said, "I'm sorry, bruh. I really am, but just know that I didn't say a word about you."

Monte offered Trey his hand, and Trey slapped the fuck out of Monte so hard that Monte fell against his mother's car.

Then Trey grabbed him by the neck and rammed his head into the car four times.

Starr screamed, "Trey, please! Please, let him go."

Trey said, "Motherfucker, I will kill you. You dumb motherfucker. You know I don't wanna get locked up for this bullshit."

Monte said, "Please, bruh, let me go."

Starr said, "Let him go, baby. Somebody is going to see you."

Trey shoved Monte to the pavement and kicked him in the side of his face. "You fuckin' idiot. Now, all because of you, I gotta watch my back."

Monte attempted to rise to his feet and Trey kicked him again. Blood shot from his nose. Trey kept stomping him until he was unconscious.

CHAPTER 69

INSIDE THE STASH HOUSE IN SANDY SPRINGS, THE SCENT OF MARIJUANA overwhelmed them. Chris led them to a bedroom where blocks of weed were piled to the ceiling. Twan said, "Goddamn, this must be at least two hundred lbs."

Black's eyes expanded. "Twan, you idiot, this is at least a thousand lbs." He turned to Chris. "How much is this?"

"Close to fifteen hundred lbs."

Black had no idea how Chris got loads of weed in this large. He didn't want to sound impressed, because he actually wasn't impressed. He had his own money, but he always wanted more.

Chris said, "Remember, man, do not harm my mother."

Black looked him in the eye and said, "Man to man, nothing is going to happen to your mama."

Chris didn't know whether to believe them or not, but there was nothing he wouldn't do to keep his mother safe.

Twan and K.B. loaded the weed up in the Expedition and Escalade that they had parked in the garage.

When they were done, Twan, K.B. and Black brought Chris into the garage. Chris was limping slowly from the shot Twan had fired into his foot. Black was walking slowly too since he was on crutches.

When they got into the garage, Black said, "Tie his bitch-ass up."

Twan and K.B. stripped him butt-naked and hogtied him.

Black took his crutch and rammed it hard into Chris's asshole. Chris hollered. Chris didn't know what having a baby felt like, but he knew there was no pain worse than what he felt right now.

"Any more drugs?"

"No."

"Money?"

"This is it."

Twan fired a shot into the back of Chris's head, his brain matter splattering on the tire of the Expedition.

Black said, "I promised you your mama was safe, but I ain't say shit about you. Thanks for the weed, homie," Black said as he stuck the crutch in the dead man's mouth

K.B. and Twan tossed Chris's body into the back of the Expedition.

CHAPTER 70

JADA HAD PREPARED CRAIG'S DINNER BY CANDLELIGHT. HE WAS sitting at the table stone-faced, not touching his vegetables or his blackened fish. She knew she could cook with the best of them. She'd cooked for him before. He looked as if somebody close to him had died. She eased behind him trying to give him a massage and he pushed her away.

"What's wrong baby?" asked Jada.

Still no answer. He looked at her but didn't say shit to her. She sat in the chair across from him and bit into her fish. Then she drank some of her sparkling water, but still he wasn't saying anything to her. She wondered if his wife had found out about his affair. He stood and walked into the den. She followed him. The remote control was on the table. He grabbed it, turned the television on to ESPN and sat down, still stone-faced.

Finally, she said, "So you're not going to tell me what the fuck is your problem?"

He glanced at her as if he wanted to say something, but he didn't speak.

"Tell me your goddamned problem."

He said nothing.

"What the fuck is your problem, Craig?"

Finally, he said, "You're my fucking problem. You are."

"And what is that supposed to mean."

"It means, I want you out of here in the morning."

"What?"

"You sold my goddamned car, Jada. You sold something that I gave you.

How in the hell did you do me like this?"

She wanted to say something, but she couldn't. Even though it wasn't true since she hadn't sold the car. She'd only signed it over to the attorney.

Jada bit down hard on her lip. Wondering how she was going to get out of this situation and wondering, how in the hell did Craig know so much?

•   •   •

To be continued.

GET A FREE eBOOK!

Enjoyed this book?
If you enjoyed this book please write a review and email it to me at
kevinelliott3@gmail.com, and get a FREE ebook.

K. Elliott Book Order Form
PO Box 12714
Charlotte NC 28220

Book Name	Quantity	Price	Shipping/ Handling	Total
Dear Summer		X $14.95	+ $3.00 per book	
Dilemma		X $14.95	+ $3.00 per book	
Entangled		X $13.95	+ $3.00 per book	
Godsend Series 1–5		X $14.95	+ $3.00 per book	
Godsend Series 6–10		X $14.95	+ $3.00 per book	
Kingpin Wifeys Vol. 1		X $14.95	+ $3.00 per book	
Kingpin Wifeys Vol. 2		X $14.95	+ $3.00 per book	
Kingpin Wifeys Vol. 3		X $14.95	+ $3.00 per book	
Kingpin Wifeys Vol. 4		X $14.95	+ $3.00 per book	
Street Fame		X $14.95	+ $3.00 per book	
Treasure Hunter		X $15.00	+ $3.00 per book	
			TOTAL	

Mailing Address

Name:

Mailing Address:

City	State	Zip

Method Of Payment

[   ] Check [   ] Money Order

Thank you for your support!

About the Author

K. ELLIOTT, AKA THE WELL FED BLACK WRITER, PENNED HIS FIRST novel, Entangled, in 2003. Although he was offered multiple signing deals, Elliott decided to found his own publishing company, Urban Lifestyle Press.

Bookstore by bookstore, street vendor by street vendor, Elliott took to the road selling his story. He did not go unnoticed, selling 50,000 units in his first year and earning a spot on the Essence Magazine Bestsellers list.

Since Entangled, Elliott has published five titles of his own and two more on behalf of authors signed to Urban Lifestyle Press. For one book, The Ski Mask Way, Elliott was selected to co-author with hip-hop superstar 50 Cent. Along the way, he has continued to look for innovative ways to push his books to his fans while keeping down his overhead.

Elliott is passionate about sharing what he has learned with aspiring authors, and has conducted learning webinars filled with information on what works best for him. He is the author of numerous best-sellers including Dilemma, Street Fame, Treasure Hunter, Dear Summer, Entangled, The Godsend Series and the hugely intriguing Kingpin Wifeys Series.

www.ingramcontent.com/pod-product-compliance
Lightning Source LLC
Chambersburg PA
CBHW070019120726
47909CB00003B/999